P9-BYS-459

Now In
November

JOSEPHINE JOHNSON

Carroll & Graf Publishers, Inc.
New York

First Carroll & Graf edition 1985

Carroll & Graf Publishers, Inc.
260 Fifth Avenue
New York, NY 10001

ISBN: 0-88184-174-9

Manufactured in the United States of America.

CONTENTS

Part One

PRELUDE AND SPRING

1

Part Two

THE LONG DROUTH

111

Part Three

YEAR'S END

211

PART ONE   PRELUDE AND SPRING

NOW in November I can see our years as a whole. This autumn is like both an end and a beginning to our lives, and those days which seemed confused with the blur of all things too near and too familiar are clear and strange now. It has been a long year, longer and more full of meaning than all those ten years that went before it. There were nights when I felt that we were moving toward some awful and hopeless hour, but when that hour came it was broken up and confused because we were too near, and I did not even quite realize that it had come.

I can look back now and see the days as one looking down on things past, and they have more shape and meaning than before. But nothing is really finished or left behind forever.

The years were all alike and blurred into one another, and the mind is a sort of sieve or quicksand, but I remember the day we came and the months afterward well enough. Too well. The roots of our life, struck in back there that March, have a queer resemblance to their branches.

The hills were bare then and swept of winter leaves, but the orchards had a living look. They were stained with the red ink of their sap and the bark tight around them as though too small to hold the new life of coming leaves. It was an old place and the land had been owned by Haldmarnes since the Civil War, but when we came no one had been living there for years. Only tenant farmers had stayed awhile and left. The land was stony, but with promise, and sheep grew fat in the pastures where rock ledges were worn back, white like stone teeth bared to frost. There were these great orchards planted up and down the hills, and when Mother saw them that first day she thought of having to gather the crop and haul the apples up this steepness, but she only said a good harvest ought to come, and the trees looked strong though old. "No market even if they bear," I remember Father said· and then,—"it's mortgaged land."

Nobody answered and the wagon went on groaning and squeaking in the ruts. Merle and I watched the jays, blue-flickering through the branches, and heard their screams. The elms were thick with buds and brown-webbed across the sky It was beautiful and barren in the pastures, and the walnuts made a kind of lavender-colored shadow, very clean. Things were strange and unrelated and made no pattern that a person could trace easily. Here was the land and the spring air full of snow melting, and yet the beginning of fear already,—this mortgage, and Father consumed in himself with sour irritation and the future dread. But Mother sat there very quiet. He had not told her the place was mortgaged, and the land at least, she had thought, was unencumbered, and sanctuary though everything else was gone. But even in the moment when she saw that this, too, was uncertain and shifting ground, something she always had—something I didn't know then and may never know—let her take it quietly. A sort of inner well of peace. Faith I guess it was. She stood a great deal and put up with much, but all without doubt or bitterness; and that she was there, believing and not shaken, or not seeming so at least, was all that we needed then to know. We could forget for the time this sense of impermanence and doubt which had come up from his words. Merle was ten then and I was fourteen, and it seemed to us that some great adventure had begun. But Father looked only at the old, year-rotted barns.

He wasn't a man made for a farmer, Arnold Haldmarne, although brought up on the land when a boy, and now returning to acres not different much from the ones he used to plough. He hadn't the resignation that a farmer has to have,—that resignation which knows how little use to hope or hate, or pray for even a bean before its appointed time. He'd left the land when he was still sixteen and gone to Boone, making himself a place in the lumber factories there. He'd saved and come up hard and slow like an oak or ash that grows with effort but is worth much more than any poplar shooting two feet high in a season. But now he was chopped back down to root again. It's a queer experience for a man to go through, to work years for security and peace, and then in a few months' time have it all dissolve into nothing; to feel the strange blankness and dark of being neither wanted nor necessary any more. Things had come slow to him and gone fast, and it made him suspicious even of the land.

We hauled our beds here in the wagon with us. The car was sold and most of the furniture gone too. We left our other life behind us as if it had not been. Only the part that was of and in us, the things we'd read and the things remembered, came with us, and the books we'd gathered through three generations but could not sell because earth was knee-deep and wading in books already. We left a world all wrong, confused, and shouting at itself, and came here to one that was no less hard and no less ready to thwart a man or cast him out, but gave him something, at least, in return. Which was more than the other one would do.

The house was old even then, not log, but boards up and down as barns are made. It was overgrown with the trumpet and wild red ivy-vines, twisted and heavy on the porch. Wild grapes were black across the well in autumn and there was an arbor of tame ones over the pump. Father found an old thrush's nest hunched up in the leafless vines and took it down so that Merle wouldn't mistake it for a new nest in spring and keep waiting for birds that never came. She filled it full of round stones and kept it up on the mantelpiece, maybe because she thought that the fire would hatch stone birds,—I didn't know. She was full of queer notions and things that never existed on earth. She seemed older sometimes than even Kerrin who was born five years ahead.

That first spring when everything was new to us I remember in two ways; one blurred with the worry and fear like a grey fog where Father was—a fog not always visible but there, and yet mixed with it this love we had for the land itself, changing and beautiful in a thousand ways each hour. I remember the second day we came was stormy with fist-big flakes of snow and a northwest wind that came down across the hills, rattling the windows until the panes were almost broken, and the snow smacked wet against the glass. We thought it an omen of what the winters here would be, but strangely it was not cold afterward, even with almost two feet of snow along the ground, and a wind that shook the hickories from branch to root and sent a trembling down through the oaks. Merle and I went down by a stony place in the woods where the rocks shelved out to make a fall, and saw the air-bubbles creeping under the ice, wriggling away with a quick and slippery dart like furtive tadpoles. Down near the crawfish shallows the slime ferns were green and fresh and the sun so hot that we walked with our coats swung open and stuffed our caps away. Much of everything, it seemed afterward, was like that beginning,—changing and so balanced between wind and sun that there was neither good nor evil that could be said to outweigh the other wholly. And even then we felt we had come to something both treacherous and kind, which could be trusted only to be inconstant, and would go its own way as though we were never born.

2

IT WAS cold that first March and the ploughing late, I remember. There are times out of those early years that I have never forgotten; words and days and things seen that lie in the mind like stone. Our lives went on without much event, and the things that happened rise up in the mind out of all proportion because of the sameness that lay around them. That first spring was like in a way to most that followed, but marked with a meaning of its own.

Kerrin complained of the raw coldness and the house was hard to keep warm enough, but I remember one day of God that came toward the last, when we lay down carefully on the grass so as not to smash the bluets, and smelled their spring-thin scent. The hills were a pale and smoky green that day, and all colors ran into and melted with each other, the red of crab branches dissolving down into lavender of shadows, but the apples had bark of bloody red and gold. We went up where the old barn was then, the one grey-shingled with sagging beams—that was in its age like a risen part of the earth itself. We ate our lunch there on the south side of its wall and sucked in the hot spring sun and the pale waterwashed blue along beyond the trees, and even Kerrin seemed less alien and odd. Dad had too much to do and could not waste his time in coming, for the getting enough to live on and eat was work sufficient itself, and if a man thought to put anything aside or to pile it up for another time, it kept his nose in the furrow and his hand on the plough even while he slept. Mother stayed back with him to eat, and we thought they were probably glad to be alone one meal at least, without all our eyes staring them up and down and noting the things they said, to remember and repeat should they ever at any time contradict themselves.

We sat on the hill and watched a bluebird searching the trees and along the fence posts, and could see a long way off into the bottom land where the creek was and the maples that followed the water, long-branched and bending down to its pools. There was a shrike in the crab branches and Kerrin said they were cruel things, impaling the field-mice and birds on locust thorns so that their feet stuck out stiff like little hands. I didn't think they were cruel things though—only natural. They reminded me of Kerrin, but this I had sense not to say aloud.

"Dad's birthday comes soon now," Merle said. "He'll be fifty-seven. We should have a party, I think. --With presents." She got up slow and shaking herself like a shaggy thing, heavy with warm sun and the food. She stood up in front of us with a round grave face.

"Where'll you get the money?" Kerrin asked. "I've got some, but you haven't any. I bought a knife that I'm going to give him."

I looked at Kerrin quick and jealous. "—Where'd you get money from?" I asked. I hadn't remembered there was a birthday coming, or thought of a thing to give, and it made me angry at her.

"It's mine, Marget. I earned it!" Kerrin shouted. "I suppose that you think I stole or borrowed!" She got up and glared down on me. She was dark all over her long thin face, and I think she hoped that I did suspect her—she wanted to feel accused of dark and secret things. I probed the earth into little holes and buried a dandelion head, embarrassed and half-afraid of what she might do to me. "I just wondered," I said, "since nobody else has any."

Kerrin drew herself stiff like a crane. Her eyes seemed almost to twitch when she got excited or thought that she had a right to be. "You ought to have shut your mouth before you talked. You don't know anything anyway!" Her liddy eyes opened fierce. She was always making scenes.

Merle clasped her fat hands together. She was anxious and uneasy and dreaded these times more than any snake or ghost. "We ought to be going back," she said. "Maybe it's later than the dishes—"

Kerrin looked angry and defiant. "What if it is? Who cares? Maybe I'm not going back a while!" She kept breaking twigs in her skinny hands.

"Kerrin," I said like a pompous fool, "it isn't always the things we want that are given us to do."

"Why don't you do them then?" Kerrin sneered.

I didn't have anything to say. I was afraid to start probing again about the knife. Nothing was changed, but the afternoon seemed cold and chilly. . . . Merle started off down the hill. She was always thinking of Mother having to do the work alone, and was always the first to start at whatever there was to be done. Something was in her, even then, that kept walking foot after foot down a straight path to some clear place, and I wished then, and still do, that there was something in me also that would march steadily in one road, instead of down here or there or somewhere else, the mind running a net of rabbit-paths that twisted and turned and doubled on themselves, pursued always by the hawk-shadow of doubt. But even though I despised myself, it seemed that earth was no less beautiful or less given to me in my littleness than to Merle who had twice as much of good in her. And it seemed unjust and strange, but would probably balance up some day.

I ran after her and Kerrin followed, not wanting to come or to stay alone. "What'll you give him, Merle?" I asked. She looked red and proud, pleased to be questioned when she knew the answer. "I'm going to give him a box," she said. "A big one for his nails and screws."

"That's wonderful," I told her. "You can make partitions in it for the sizes, and stain it some." But I didn't see how she was going to do it at all.

"What're you going to give him?" Kerrin asked me.

"Everyone ought to have something anyway. It doesn't have to be awfully much."

"You'll see," I said. In my heart I didn't think that it *would* be much. I wondered if maybe it wouldn't be anything at all. I wasn't much good at making things.

We went slow in the hot sun. Merle was quiet, thinking, I guess, of all the chickens whose nests still had to be filled, and of the lame one who broke all her eggs but wanted so steadfastly to hatch that it was pitiful, though Merle hated her stupidness and the egg-stuck, smelly hay. It was almost two, and it seemed as if doing nothing at all took up time faster and more unknowing of what it swallowed than work had ever done. We walked up the cow-path where the ground was dry and warm, and alongside the thistles coming up. We could see Dad ploughing again already and robins come down in the furrows but keeping a long way off from the plough. There was a blue-smoke smell from burning brush and a warm haze in the air. Merle walked first, round and with a clean skin, and her mouth full of the one left piece of bread, and her hair messed up and woolly in the back; and then I came, not looking comparable to much of anything, with a brown dress on and beggar-lice seeds in my stockings; and then Kerrin straggled along behind, acting as though she might leave us any minute. She had reddish hair cut off in a bang, and her arms like two flat laths hung down loose from her shoulders, but her face was much sharper and more interesting than ours. She was stronger, too, and thought she could plough if Father'd let her. But he thought that a girl could never learn how and would only mess the field. "You help your mother, girls," he'd say. "You help your mother." He hired a man to work for a while and Kerrin was angry, felt things pounding in her, impotent and suppressed, and was sullen and lowering as the young bulls are. "He thinks I can't do anything!" she'd shout at Mother. "He treats me as if I were still two. Why don't you do something about it? Why don't you make him see?"

"He'll see after a while," Mother said. "I think he'll see pretty soon."

"Why don't you tell him though?" Kerrin'd say. "Why do you always wait so long about everything? You treat him like he was God Himself!" She'd end that way each time and slam a door somewhere while we pretended not to hear and would go on with what we did, only sick and drawn inside with hate. And for Mother who took things hard and quiet and lived in the lives of other people as though they were her own, it was like being bruised inside each time. I'd hear her suggesting things to Father in a quiet and hesitating way, and if he were tired he would be angry, or if in the rare times when he was pleased about something—about Merle's fat cheeks that seemed to glow in wind, or about some clever thing she had said—he would laugh but never agree at once or let her know she had changed his mind. It was hard for her to bring things up at the times when he was pleased or sitting down quietly, because he had so few of these intervals, and it seemed like torturing him. We would walk carefully, praying the moment to last longer, to stretch out into an hour, and sometimes Mother would let the chance go past for the sake of peace, although there was much that she felt unjust, and had pestilent worries of her own she would like to have burdened on him.

When we came back that day we saw Mother had all of the old potatoes spread on the cistern-top and was cutting them up for seed. She looked thin and lumpy and her hair was wound in a braided ball behind. She was round-cheeked and young-looking, though, and glad to see us—which used to puzzle me sometimes, even then, thinking that fourteen years of us should have made her more chary and doubtful of our company.

"We had a good time," Merle said, "and the lunch was good." She stuck out some oozy dandelion stems curled together with spit, and plastered them on behind at the bottom of Mother's knot.

"They look beautiful," Kerrin said. "They look like worms." She started to cut up potatoes, very fast and neatly, but Merle paid no attention and nobody else did either. I thought that it served her right, and Mother only laughed. Mother never talked much herself, but listened to everything that was said, and it made us feel there was reason in talking because she was there to hear. Nobody else we had ever met cared as much for all of the things that there were to know and be talked about—the wheeling of planets and the meaning of bonds, or the kind of salts that the chickens needed and the names of the great Victorian poets.

We hacked the potatoes for a long time, and quiet. The sun was still warm, and slow in moving. I thought about Kerrin and the money, and wondered when she had earned it for the knife, and thought most likely she simply had taken it (which was so), but forgot this in watching a grey hawk skimming along the oaks, and forgot it in wondering what supper was going to be. It was as if sun had slowed up everything and pressed us out calmer and more smooth. For a little while, at least.

3

THAT year we had planned for his birthday three weeks ahead. But it was all strange around us—the land and the people were—and we could not ask anyone but ourselves to come. There were the Rathmans Father knew,—Old Man Rathman and his wife and their three sons like three big bulls, and one daughter with a round fat face; Dad used to go and eat with them sometimes on Saturdays. Almost any time that he went, he said, they were at the table, starting or finishing one of their five meals, and smell of coffee seemed a part of the house itself, soaked in the walls and mingled with the kraut. Old Mrs. Rathman spent all her life between table and stove, and when she went outside it was only to bring things in to put on the stove awhile and then on the table and from there into the three boys and Joseph Rathman and sometimes into herself. Dad liked Old Rathman and named the first calf after his girl Hilda, instead of for one of us (not that we minded much, it being ugly and one-horned and a nasty purple); but we were afraid of the old man because his eyes seemed to mock us, to have some hidden secret or scandal about us and to feel contempt. I know now that it was only his way and that he liked us because we were healthy-looking and children. But we were afraid to ask him then. Merle said that she might forget her poem and Kerrin said they might not like our food, and I said nothing but was glad they had decided this way. I had a horror of unfamiliar people, but did not want blame should it turn out in the end that it might have been better if we'd asked them (which was always the way I did, so that they thought me good-natured when I really was nothing but a coward).

The Rathmans were the only ones near us on the north, but down to the south the Ramseys lived on a thin and brush-filled farm. The Ramseys were negroes and the place had a starved and rocky look.

All of the animals were gaunt and bony, and even the pigs looked empty like a balloon gone slack;—even the little shoats were black and small with huge, fox-pointed ears. Christian Ramsey was tall and thin with a soiled color, and his wife was named Lucia. They owned a pack of spotted and ghostly hounds, and they had five children—three of their own, and two adopted—one that was almost white but with great lips, and they had not wanted it but nobody else did either, so they kept the child and, Father said, treated it better than the rest, either from fear or pity, he never could quite decide. But we could not ask the Ramseys, nor would they have wanted to come if we had. And the farmers beyond were only names.

We planned the party ourselves, how it was to be and what was to be made, and I taught Merle a long poem to say, and kept her in the chicken house for an hour a day sitting on the bran bin to recite it off by heart. We called it a ballad and it was an awful thing, but the words sounded rhyming at the end and there was a story in it, so it may have been one after all. Kerrin and I made it up and it ended with a death, but since Father wanted to put away all thought of death and never would let us speak of it, I left out the end in teaching it to her. Kerrin did not know this, though, because Merle would not learn it from her or be alone with her since the time she was locked in the potato cellar and left in the dark for hours. But she trusted me so much that sometimes it felt like a heavy weight on the shoulders, although wonderful and something like being God. She did not mind having to learn it, and sat there with her black-ribbed legs dangling over the barrel brim, her fat cheeks red with cold, and a piece of damp hair stuck out from under the cap with the big knob on its peak. She'd say it over nine times or ten with gusto, and then the rest of the times with patience and precision. It was about a farmer, and we hoped that Father would laugh because it was supposed to be funny in some places, but we knew that Mother would anyway. Merle was excited about it and kept counting off the days, and would look at me in a full and secret way.

Kerrin wouldn't tell us what it was she was going to do, but went off each day by herself in the woods. "It's going to be good," was all she'd say. "You-all will be shamed." Between milking and the supper she would be gone off alone and come back sometimes singing. She had a good voice, but it was too loud and shouting and made her reluctant of people hearing it, and she would stop when she came up past the barn. . . . As for me, I thought to make Dad a clay basket like the Indians did and stained with something—I didn't quite know what, beet-juice or ink perhaps—and give it to him in place of the rusty tin he used for carrying up the eggs. I spent days making it. First half-bushel size, and clay on a wire to make the handle that went shattering into bits as soon as lifted. But I made it over again three times and each time smaller, till finally it was firm and held together but was scarcely big enough to carry even a sparrow egg inside. Still, it looked like a basket anyway, and I wished it was for Mother, knowing that she would like anything we made,—even a pillow that Merle had stuffed with chicken feathers not so clean and musty-smelling. It was nice, though, to think of Dad's getting it, because it was a good pot and stained with a design of red things that were something like herons, only the juice had spread and blurred their edges around,—and because he was harder to please and so seemed more kindly when he was.

I liked the hour I spent there each day by the bank with the faint clay-cold smell of the water; there were small holes all along the edge, which might have been borings of a woodcock's bill, but spiders hid in them and caught the cabbage-butterflies that came in thin and yellow clouds to suck the clay. Sometimes I'd come down in the middle of the mornings, and hear the frost dripping off the sycamores and woodpecker's tap along the bark, because it was so quiet; and twice a red fox sneaked across the road.

But one time I heard Kerrin go by singing to herself. She couldn't see me underneath the bank, and when the singing had gotten farther off—it was about Rizpah and her son hung up in chains—I took off my cap so that the knob wouldn't come up first, and stuck my head over the bank and saw her running and singing. Her red hair was wild and not covered up as it should have been because spring is the dangerous weather, Father said. (He never went without a hat on top of his head, although what good a man's hat did I couldn't see,—leaving his ears to blow about exposed.) I almost called out and told her she should have put something on her head, but the words stayed in my mouth, and she went off around the hill. I felt queer, seeing her alone that way. Something about the way she ran and sang, as though not a person like us any more. Kerrin had never been like us much, even before, in other ways. She did things sudden and wildly, or not at all, and ate sometimes like a dog starved out and savage, chewing and mumbling, and at other times would only pick at her food and stare out the window while Merle and I ate patiently all that was put in front of us. She'd sleep at odd times and hours, stretched out like a lynx in sun, and creep out of the house at night to wander around in the marshes. I knew because I had seen her come sneaking back at dawn, with her feet and legs half-frozen and covered with frosty mud. And this time she seemed more strange than ever, as though not belonging even to herself. I felt queer. I didn't know what it was then, but it was the beginning of fear. Fear that life wasn't safe and comfortable, or even just tight and hard, but that there was an edge of darkness which was neither, and was something which no one could ever explain or understand. And that day I left the pot unfinished, and went back to the house where things, if not always good, were plain enough, at least, and not hard to understand.

Dad's birthday was in April on the ninth, but we

were ready a long time before, and the days, though full and overfull, seemed to move no faster than a stone. Merle did not ask Is this the day? each morning, but Mother could see how she was fearful of not recognizing it, and so taught her how to mark the days on the calendar each night. We planned what we should give him for supper, and wished that they could be things we had raised ourselves, but the sweet potatoes and Irish were still unborn and no vegetable more than barely underground as yet. But there were to be corn-pudding piles and a three-layered cake oozed out with icing and as many candles as it would hold, but not fifty-seven as there should have been or the cake would have slumped and fallen flat; though Merle said we ought to stick them around the sides to make it look like a porcupine on fire. Kerrin told her it couldn't be done and to leave baking to those who knew about it;—by which she didn't mean me, I guess, since the apple bullets-of-dough I made one night, nor herself either, because though liking to spade and heave earth around, she had no interest in what came out of it, and broke the carrots off instead of pulling them with persuasion or troweling.

—But she probably meant that Mother would do the best, which was true enough in more ways than cooking.

4

THE ninth of April came on a day of corn ploughing. We had battered about all night scarcely asleep, and so heard Dad get up as he always did at four, and supposed that his heart was pounding like ours. It was a queer day outside, I remember—thunder-storms and a hot sun coming between them and a wind shifting to the north with coldness, and there were long streaks of light across the wild plums that were about to flower. . . . The cake was beautiful and high, and the icing dripped out from the layers. Kerrin ate the part run out around the plate but did not break at the crust, and it looked like the tower of Babel with its layers dwindling into a muffin on the top.

At six that evening Dad came in and shouted out, "Where's the food, you women?" and sounded so young and cheerful that we climbed on him as we had not done in weeks. Mother looked suddenly younger, too and Cale barked loud as he would at some stranger. She brought in the ham stuck about with cloves, and the brown-sugar smell filled the room and moved out the dark spring coldness that had crawled in through the window cracks. "I'm going to put soybeans up in the north field," Father said. "They're cheap and nourishing."

"You ought to hire a boy to help in the planting," Mother said, "—someone with more sense than these around." Father looked at her as though she were one of us talking. "Max Rathman's good enough," he said. "What's wrong with Max? A man doesn't need to plant by textbook, Willa." I saw him looking at Merle, and saw she was feeding Cale with a piece of ham, shoving it down his mouth with her fat rough hands; and there were words in Dad's throat ready to come charging up, but they stayed in his mouth and did not come this time. "Max is good enough for a while, I guess," Mother said very fast. She shook her head at Merle, but not till he'd looked away. "Let's bring the cake in now," I whispered. I wanted to light the candles and help her to carry it in, because I had made a part—not much, but sprinkling raisins on here and there. Merle kept watching me to know if it was time to say the poem, and her eyes kept following me about with the question. Then I saw Kerrin take a big piece of uneaten bread and sneak it down to Cale, and I looked at Father and saw the words that he hadn't said all ready to rush out on her. He got red, but only a heavy sigh came out. "What's the matter?" Mother asked. She was out in the closet where the cake was hidden, but heard the sound and silence that came after. "It's a crumb got stuck," I said. I was trembling inside and afraid, but nothing happened. Then we let Merle bring the cake in on its platter, and her face looked like a big candle itself, looming above the little flames, and Dad grinned but didn't shout as we thought he should.

He cut us big slices, firm and wedge-shaped like the tall pieces of a pie, and a bigger one for Mother, and then we thought it was time for the presents to be given. Merle jumped up and looked at me eager, with her mouth all shaped and ready to begin, but I shook my head because I thought maybe Kerrin would like to be the first, and besides I was tormented with curiosity to know what it was that she'd been doing. And afterward I wished that God had sewed up my mouth, because of the look on Merle's face, trusting and disappointed. "You be the first one, Kerrin," I said. Father looked pleased but puzzled and wondering what was to come. Kerrin got up, fierce and excited in hei eyes, and pulled a small heavy thing out of her sweater pocket. She held it out toward him but kept her fingers still on it, and we could see that it was a folded knife tipped with silver on the end. "This is supposed to be your present, Dad." She sounded excited and full of pride. "Watch what I've learned to do—taught myself how to do it!" She opened the knife and aimed at a brown spot on the wall, a little spot hardly big enough to see and high up across the room. "Look out!" Dad shouted. "Stop!" He shoved back his chair and tried to snatch the knife, but jerked at her arm instead. Merle and I screamed out, and the knife went wild, straight at old Cale's blind head, and slashed across his nose. "God damn you!" Father shouted. He grabbed at Kerrin and knocked her back against the wall. Merle started to cry and Kerrin screamed out some horrible things. Only Mother had sense enough to run to Cale and slop at his nose with water. But he growled and snapped at her with his mouth full of red foam, so that she couldn't get near enough to help him. Then Father grabbed him from behind and held his mouth so he couldn't bite her.

The cut was deep and slashed back in his head, and it bled as if every vein were opened. I stood holding on hard to Merle and trying to stop her howls, and Kerrin was on her knees by Mother, trying to sop up the blood, but Dad knocked her away and roared at her to get out and leave the room. It was terrible—the way she went out in a black rage, crying, with her hands clenched and her eyes—I was scared and Merle screamed when we saw her eyes and the awful hate in them. She slammed the door and rushed out in the dark, though it was beginning to rain and a cold wind had come up. I stood there dumb, not knowing what to do or say, and Merle kept on crying. Then Dad said, "It's no use." He picked Cale up and started out toward the door. "The girl's killed him," he said. They went outside, Mother still holding the cloth around Cale's mouth, and we heard her tell Dad that it was he who had shaken Kerrin's arm. But the door slammed after and we could not hear his answer except as a loud and angry sound.

Merle and I stayed, looking at the broken-up cake and the blood, and after a few minutes she stopped crying and was quiet. Then we went to the door and listened, and over the wind heard two thumps of a gun and then only the sound of rain running down the gutters. . . . "Let's go shut the chickens up," I said. I took the lantern down, and Merle put Mother's sweater on. She looked so sad and patient with the sweater hanging down around her ankles and her fat cheeks streaked with tears and icing that I thought my heart would crack.

It was cold and quiet out in the chicken house, and the new straw had a clean smell to it. We could hear the chickens moving and churring in their sleep. There was a pile of weed hay in one corner, and we sat there with the lantern down on the floor in front. Rain made a slow and washing sound on the window glass, and we heard a small rustle of mice. We felt tired and sick, but out here in the dark with only mice sounds and the slide of rain things seemed less terrible and vile.

"Where do you think that Kerrin went?" Merle whispered to me after a while.

"I don't know," I said. "But she'll come back sometime soon, I guess." I was empty of tears and could not cry even when I thought about old Cale. I hoped that they would not bury him out in the pasture or in some bare and ugly place. And I thought about poor Kerrin, too, stumbling and hiding somewhere in the rain, angry and sick and raging like the devil.

"I guess there won't be any more party," Merle said. She sat pushed up tight against me, her round hands clasped together looking like mittens in each other.

"No more tonight," I said. "Maybe tomorrow or some other day we'll finish." But I knew it would never be the same. And after what seemed a long time to us because the dark was so still, we picked up the lantern and crept back to the house.

5

THOSE years went slowly for us. Slow because heavy with the weight of things done, and the greater weight of things unfinished and still to be learned. The seasons washed one into another and were never still, but there was no swiftness nor anything but calm and gradual change. Sometimes not even that, but a shifting back and forth of seasons . . . long stretches of rain in the December mud, and a wind like April over winter snow . . . late pea-vines springing up at Thanksgiving, and marsh-violets in the sleet, and at times the orchards would be white in autumn, the trees wasting their strength before the spring. And there was the double life, the two parts not within each other nor even parallel. The one made up of things done day after day with comfort and soberness, hard sometimes but solid—things you could lay your hands on and feel that they were there: the saucepans and heavy dishes, the thick cups and the five beds to be made—things without any more mystery than the noon sun had. The open life and the one that was greater of the two, calm, prosaic . . . rational. And there was the inner walking on the edge of darkness, the peering into black doorways . . . the unrevealed answer which must be somewhere, and yet might not be even present or hidden in that darkness . . . this under-life which when traced or held to was not there, and yet kept coming back and thrust up like an iron dike through the solid layers of the sane and understood. The moment of self-searching, of standing under the oaks at night and asking—What? Who? What am I? . . . and the moment of feeling the self gone, lost or never existent. Where am I, God? . . . the terrible desire to understand . . . the moment of realization that there are some things that are neither bad nor good, nor ever to be classified . . . the strangeness that Kerrin had . . . things that like shards of a meteorite imply the presence of worlds beyond comprehension or understanding. And there was the desire for source—the desire to understand cause, which is the heart-root of religion, and led the mind through such devious and dark tunnels, and brought it out nowhere. These years marked by the dark torment of adolescence—that time when a fallen nail unlifted or a tuft of sheep's wool is torture at night with fear and accusation. When dreams are portent or promise, and there is meaning and symbol in the crossing of two branches or a shadow's length. . . . But all the time in the back of these things there was the hill-quiet and the stony pastures, and sometimes they made me ashamed of being what I was—human and full of a thousand wormy thoughts and selfishness, but more often they were like hands to heal.

6

IN MARCH of this year–ten years since the day we came—there were tin-grey clouds and cold winds, and the white ash of orchard fires was blown east and scattered. But no rain had come since the first of February. "This year will have to be different," I thought. "We've scrabbled and prayed too long for it to end as the others have." The debt was still like a bottomless swamp unfilled, where we had gone year after year, throwing in hours of heat and the wrenching on stony land, only to see them swallowed up and then to creep back and begin again. I felt sure somehow that this year would end differently and better, and not be merely a shift of seasons that left us still bound and waiting. We had gone too long in a fog of hope.

My father's life had been a sort of fierce crawling to rid us of debt before that time when even the effort would be too heavy for him. He wanted some safety for us, freedom from that fear and doubt he had always known himself. And he wanted time to look around and be still. He loved the land in a proud, owned way,—only because it was his, and for what it would mean to us; not in the way that Merle and I did, and still do. To us it was a thing loved for its own sake, giving a sort of ecstasy and healing (high words, but even they are too pale), and we felt a nameless, not wholly understood love. But the land was all Father's life then. The whole weight of his ambition, the hope and sanity of his mind rested on the same ground he walked. This heavy, complaining labor with doubtful profit was almost the only visible sign of love he had ever showed us. But it was one that I'd never doubted.

Father was like Kerrin in that he couldn't see the masterpiece of a maggot or be satisfied with the shadow of a leaf, in which ways we were older than he was, but young in being so blind we could not see the heaviness of his responsibility or know the probe of that fear which made him want security at the expense of our happiness.—I think sometimes that he would have been a milder, more patient man had there been some sons instead of nothing but girls' talk all the time and women-voices. Life's lonely enough and isolated enough without the thick wall of kind to make it go even darker. Later we did not talk so much, but in the first years we were like a bunch of guineas, cackling and squawking at all hours. It irritated him to have us picking and pecking at lives of other people, and telling the things we'd heard. "Shut up!" he'd shout.—"Shut up and keep out of others' business!" And at times we had hated him for it. He felt too that we blamed him because there was nothing left but this land out of everything he had piled together for years; but the truth was that we never thought about this, and were glad that the place was old and stony and full of uncleared woods. Nor did Mother blame him either in word or mind. The only place she wanted to be was where Father was, whether this place was Eden or Sheol itself, and what form it took didn't matter much. But he was so raw in mind himself that he suspected us all.

We never seemed able to make much over. All that we saved above what it cost to live—and live by mouth and mind only, with nothing new but the seasons or thoughts we had—all went into the mortgage-debt. It would have taken so little to make us happy. A little more rest, a little more money—it was the nearness that tormented. The nearness to life the way we wanted it. And things that have cost more than they're worth leave a bitter taste. A taste of salt and sweat.

The spring crept up slowly this year; tide-like receded. Green crosiers of the ferns again and the mandrakes humping up like toadstools in the grass. I got tired as a rag sometimes and would not have minded being run through with a locust thorn and left for the shrikes to pick at. What use all this in the end? The hope worn on indefinitely . . . the desire never fulfilled . . . four o'clock and the ice-grey mornings . . . the cows and dark . . . the cans enormous in the foggy lamplight . . . day come up cold and windy . . . Max sullen as a red clod . . . the endless cooking . . . the sour rim of pails . . . Father's grey shirts soaking all day in water. . . . There seemed no answer, and the answer lay only in forgetting.

But the days were warm sometimes. Spring came first to the air, and then to the life of things. The elm trees were green like sulphur smoke, or dust from a dry old fungus-ball; the wild ginger hard-packed still on its roots, but green with a silver mold, and in the ravine I found a moccasin snake coiled and hating, while the cold spring water flowed over his skin, over and over until I grew almost chilled with seeing it. The ground was hard. Things struggled up with their heads bent over. Father began to plough, and cut farther into the woods this year. Acres of wild phlox turned to corn. There was no use to say anything. Not even Merle did any more. Four trees came down, two pin-oaks and some sycamores, and the oaks had a queer and oily smell. No peaches this year. Blossoms stuck scrappily, one or two on a branch; but the apple buds were thick, and the pear trees covered. "A good year," we said, "—if nothing happens." (I wondered if anywhere on earth men could say such and such will be, with certainty. No farmer ever could.) One good year and the land would be ours again. I could imagine life free of this weight, so wonderful that only to be alive would be in itself enough. But hope was all we had then; not even belief—unless hope so strong and obstinate that nothing can root it out is called a faith.

It was queer how little rain came that month, and we thought that the next would bring a flood.

7

WHEN Kerrin's school closed in April this year, I dreaded the thought of her being home all day. It seemed to me even then, eight months ago, that there was something more inerasably wrong with her than just a fierce selfishness and discontent. This teaching only held back awhile the black tide of something that had its beginning with her birth. Four years after we came, she had started to teach at the Union County school, although she was only nineteen then and there were some on the board who said it was wrong to have her even as only a substitute for Ally Hines. It wasn't her age they minded so much, but we never had joined the church; and there was some talk of her "not being the one for the place," but it dwindled into a mild nothing. Kerrin was good as a teacher and worked much harder than Ally Hines, with her cancerous bones and cough, had ever been able to. Ally had come down sick in the middle of the year, and Kerrin had asked for the place herself. The board would never have thought or considered her of their own accord, but when they heard she was through with high school, which was all that Ally herself had done, they took her for lack of knowing what else to do and being confused with Ally's sickness as a thing not reckoned on in their almanacs. We were glad, not only because of the money—which Kerrin kept to herself, knowing it gave her a kind of power even though she might have to lend it sometime,—but glad because it took her away from home.

Even when she was quiet or reading, I could never

find rest where Kerrin was. None of us could. Only out in the fields was there any peace when she was at home. I would come in the house sometimes and, without seeing or hearing, know she was there, and know too when she was gone without hearing her go. No matter in what sort of mood she was—and there were times when Kerrin was almost fiercely happy and kind—the tautness was never gone, the fear of what she might say or do.

She made a good teacher, good because she understood all those lumpy children in so far as any but God could understand them, I guess, and held them all to her with a kind of hard leniency and discipline. She succeeded because she really cared about them and thought it important that they should know the states and the laws and the years in which things happened or died, although not caring if she forgot it all forever, herself. She believed that for some reason it was important and valuable for them to know 1066 and the mystery of square root, and never asked herself exactly why and so was able to teach them well and thoroughly. There's a driving force—an energy lying in blindness—which is never known by those wondering and open-minded ones who are led by thought into doubt, and from there through all the stages of futility and despair until they are paralyzed to point out one way or the other even to children who haven't the sense to sneer. But Kerrin, who riddled all laws herself, took a fanatic delight in shoving down law and order into their placid throats, amiably open wide and gaping. The children loved her, and sometimes she brought them home after school, one or two at a time, for no reason except that they asked her to. If they were little boys that came, Father would stop his work and come up to talk with them in an eager, hearty way, pointing out the pig houses or the water-pump by the pond, and laugh at whatever they said, no matter whether their words were smart or foolish. Kerrin herself liked the boys better because their faces were not so stupid and their minds clicked faster. The girls were already vacant wives, she said, —not stolid, their tongues slapping around like wheels, but already bounded tight with convention, a thick wall between them and the unknown things; nor was it in Kerrin to see and point out a way, or break a hole that these children could nose through and escape. "—Hillbillies and tenant farmers," she said. "No Lincoln'll ever come out of these. Smart enough to be even school-teachers, maybe, repeating the things they've read. Why should I try for more? They only want to know enough so they can clerk in a store some place and ride in a Ford on Sundays. Want to be able to read the magazines and catalogues. If they're looking for more, they can go some place else and get it!—And none of them ever will. . . ."

It was true and it wasn't true—what she said about the children. People weren't born and fastened to earth any more. They came and went, returning and leaving, not like a tide but in scattered ways and times. People came back to the land as we had come, after years of another life, bringing with them a newness to old things, a different seeing from the sight of men born with the sound of calves' bawling in their ears and the taste of mud in their mouths from the beginning. There was no solitude utterly unpierced, no isolation complete any longer—except for the final one of self. If Kerrin had chosen to point out the myriad facets of life, the strangeness of breath itself, she might not have left them so blind and narrow, even if they had been as indifferent as she thought. But maybe she herself didn't see these things, and was blind and gaping, too, which made her restless and full of uncertain angry moods, and above all lonely.

I hoped that this year she would find enough work to keep her quiet, and wished that August with schools beginning was not so far, although God knows we needed her help enough. She had been of more use to Father than even she herself realized, and things had taken him twice as long while she was away at school. He was slow and fumbled the harness, jerked and thumped at the horses until they pounded the walls. Kerrin used to do it all for him, shoving the bits in swift and angry, but with no hesitation or fumbling tries. A sort of contemptuous certainty. She used to feed them at noon and toss in corn, kind and yet viciously, damning their eagerness. The stalls got muck-deep and moldy when she was gone, and Father left them because there was little time. But this year when school closed, she seemed to forget all the things she used to do, and it was only by nagging that we made her work.

I wished that all the strength which she spent in hate and in searching for something she did not even name to herself had been ours to use. But I knew that strength alone would never have helped us much, and even if we had raised nine farms we would have had less than an acre's return in money. Kerrin herself never cared whether or not this slough of debt was filled, and to her the land was only a place to stay in, and as lonely as peaks or islands are.

She spent most of her time now, as she used to do when we were children, reading—it seemed, almost everything that was piled up there on the shelves. She would lie with her hard brown face casting a shadow on the page, and go through the books that the grandfathers used to own—old books that had page after page without a new paragraph or picture, and filled with philosophies obscure and gloomy as were the bindings, but even more durable perhaps. She spent hours in reading them over and did not stop, as Merle and I did, at a certain page or time, or stop to do dishes and scrabble in earth to make a garden. She was never law or time bound, or thinking of how her eyes might hurt; and she had a faith that was almost religious in believing a thing must be so if a man would bother to write it out seriously and bind it in a book.

Even if we had had more money, I doubt that Kerrin would have been satisfied. She carried the root of her unrest with her, a root not the kind that pushed the self on and up to accomplishment and fed it with a desire, but a poisoned thing that wasted its strength in pushing down here and there, and found only a shallow soil or one full of rocks wherever planted. I knew that she wanted love,—not anything we could give her, frugal and spinsterly, nor Father's (having long ago stopped even hoping for it), but some man's love in which she could see this image she had of herself reflected and thus becoming half-true. I knew it was this fierce restlessness, this desire and hunger that had led her—even after teaching school all day, and carrying up milk at night, and finishing all those things accumulated and undone as though tipped there from the day like a rubbish heap of the hours' leavings—to go out fox-hunting at night with the farmers, or walk alone, tramping the marsh grass and weeds or along the dim rutted roads until morning. I would crouch cold on these nights in bed or at the window, driven by some obsession to see her come and go, and could not sleep until the empty moonpatch on her bed was broken and I could see the light on her bony and polished arms.

I felt empty and thirsty, too, sometimes, dreaming

wild and impossible dreams, but was driven easily from them by the pattern of a shadow or a pot on the stove, and driven from them too by a wry sense of humor that made my mind leap always to see the vision's end. Not even on April nights heavy with grape smell, or in the moving of shadow-leaves could my mind forget the inevitable noon.

8

ON FATHER'S birthday this year, I walked up near to the old stone fence where we'd buried Cale. Merle and I had piled some of its rocks in a sort of cairn on top of his grave, and planted wild ginger there. We used to see Kerrin going up this hill-path sometimes, and once, years ago, we found her crying on top of the cairn and sneaked away, pretending not to see. It seemed queer to us who had never cried afterward but had loved him so much when alive—much more than she had, we thought. But now I'm not sure of it.—Kerrin had a strange way of not seeming to notice things or care about them, but years later we'd find the feeling was there, living and fierce, under a thin slab of indifference.

The stones were toppled over and wrenched apart by roots, but the wild ginger still covered it like the leaves of enormous ivy. I saw Kerrin down on the road below me, and wondered if she would come here to the cairn. She was curiously sentimental in some ways and played small parts for her own sake even when no one could see her, and it would have been like her to come here on this day. She went on past to the barn, though, and did not look up or turn.

We did not celebrate Father's birthday any more, but I would have liked to bring him back something from the woods, some foolish thing like a bud or stone, to make him know that I had remembered the day. But it was hard to give trivial things, and I wondered if after all I was glad that he was born and had any reason to make the day seem a special thing. If I had spent money for a present he would have been anxious over the cost and suspicious as always, demanding to know where it came from, and seeing the farm sold under our feet for the sake of a ten-cent tie.

We let this day go by without saying much, and I think he himself had forgotten the meaning of it;

but there was one thing at least this year that set it apart again from other days.

Father came up tired that night while Merle was peeling potatoes, cutting the skins off thick and stoutly, her mind full as always of some strange thing she had thought or memorized, and not noticing what she did. He smiled at her absently, more out of habit left from the days when she was small and her hair stood up rough and matted like weedy grass behind, than from any feeling of kindliness left now. He turned toward Mother and threw his hat on the table, mopped at his damp and rutted face. "Max isn't coming back," he said. "It seems not to pay to work for me!" He looked at Mother as if it were she who had driven Max off or else had failed through some fault to hold him here.

It wasn't his bitter voice she noticed, though, or even the blame. All her concern was for the meaning of what he'd said. What it would mean to him and Max. "What's the matter, Arnold?" she asked. "What's wrong with Max?" She saw him sick, hurt to death, wagon-pitched and already dying. She lived in the lives of others as though she hadn't one of her own.

"Nothing's wrong with Max," Father said. "He's gone where he'll get more pay. Gone to do road-work, and left me flat. I paid him for ploughing and was going to do corn on shares. I ain't the money to pay a man for that. Someone'll have to do it on shares."

"Maybe you could sell it," Mother said. "Pay someone to help and sell the corn this fall."

Father laughed. A sound more like a snort or sneer, as though he were glad to have her mistaken. "If it's good," he said, "so'll everyone else's be. Land'll be drowned in corn.—How's a man to know?" he burst out, exasperated. "You ought to be able to sell all the stuff you raise! Somebody needs it. A farm ought to pay as good as a road. No road's going to feed a man!" He looked old—old and childish at the same time. As if he might burst out crying soon. It was awful—the rage he felt; but it wasn't the anger so much as the despair that made us afraid.

"Maybe Christian Ramsey could come," Mother suggested. She put out the words with doubt, feeling her way along his mind.

"Christian's swamped under now. Got all his creek-bottom full. What'd he do with ten acres more?" He slapped the words at her raw.

"Grant Koven might do it then," Mother said. She knew that nothing was ever as overwhelming or final as he seemed to think,—that if he would wait, instead of shouting, there'd be less to shout over in the end.

"No," Father said. He shoved her suggestions away as though they were stupid thoughts that had come to him hours ago and been found of no use. He stared at his hands. Sullen and tired, the anger going out. Then he jerked his head toward Merle, saw the potatoes half-peeled with their skins still patched around, and asked when supper was going to be. "If you'd have it any time soon," he muttered, "I'd make it over to Kovens' tonight."

I was glad that Kerrin didn't come in that time. She made it a point to stay away, out in the barns or field, till supper was ready; and sometimes didn't come even then, but ate by herself, secret and ravenously. She would scoop the syrup of sweet potatoes out of the dish with her hands, and wipe out the roasting-pan with pieces of bread hacked off and ragged. Father stopped asking about her after a while and looked at her doubtfully when she did come in, suspecting her of some hidden reason. I never got used to his sick impatience, and felt racked all the time with hate and pity. Even before, when we were younger, I'd sit and watch him sometimes at the table, when he sat there eating and leaving things on his plate and not saying much, with the tired look on his face that made me want to cry at times, although I was quick to hate him when he would turn on us suddenly and shout out: "Eat your dinner, you girls! Stop messing with your food!" But all the time I would feel us there on his shoulders, heavy as stone on his mind—all four of our lives to carry everywhere. And no money.

Kerrin said once he made her think of the mad King Lear, and wondered if after all the daughters were wholly wrong. "He was a wild old man and half-mad already. How could they reason with one like that?" she'd ask. She read the play with a sort of gloomy pleasure, and memorized pages off by heart—mostly the cold and rational words of Goneril, and then, more for the sound than anything else, the howling of Edgar on the heath. I was glad that she wasn't here, watching and thinking about him, this time while Father sat at the table and drummed with his fingers on the cloth, not hungry but tired and impatient.

When supper was done, he left for the Kovens' early.

I had never seen Grant, but Merle had, a long time ago when she was still little and he came through hunting a horse he'd lost. She didn't remember much except that the one he rode was tired, and he left it out by the barn, going away on foot. She gave it some water, and when he came back he took what was left and washed off its head and sides. His hands were as big as shovels, she said, but hadn't noticed much else. Kerrin would have remembered everything; she'd have remembered even the things he wore and whatever he'd said and a lot that he didn't say. Grant was about thirty-one, Mother said, and had been away from home for five years, working on ranches and in the mines after he'd finished school, but had come back now to his father's place. Bernard Koven had been a minister once, then he bought this land of his and went back to farming while he still had a tithe saved up and breath to make use of it. They owned only pasture land, not fit for much but mullein plants and grazing, and kept both steers and hogs. They did no dairying, or any of all those things that Father had started and was breaking his back to keep on doing —each by itself too much for one man alone.

I went down to the wood-pond by myself that night. It was cold and windy. Too cold almost for rain. The frogs sang loud enough to deafen, but stopped dead when I came. They sounded like old women cackling in the water. I stopped to listen, but could think of nothing except whether or not Grant would come, and wondered if he would be a man like Father. It was hard to think of another kind, and yet harder to think of him as young. It seemed strange, too, that we would have someone different to live with us, a person with knowledge that was taught, and one who had gone beyond this county and state, learning things by sight instead of just reading about them. Father had done this, too, but now it was as though these ten years of farming had blotted out all that was behind, and he was only a little different from those around us—the Ramseys and Huttons and Mayers who knew a great deal but saw it only from this one land-bound side.

It was miserably cold. Ground even at the pond-edge hard. No spring about anything, and even the wild plums dim like a dirty web. I felt excited, though, and full of a kind of nameless hope. This year, I thought, will be different . . . better.

I stood there long enough for the frogs to think I

had gone, and they started up again, grunting and rumbling a long way apart;—and then came the shrill, insane chorus, thrust up like spears of sound, but guttering away again into a silence.

9

I WONDERED a lot about Grant in those days before he came. Merle seemed only mildly interested, though, and hoped that he wouldn't eat very much. Kerrin said nothing at all about him and may not even have known that he was to come. She was never around when things were told, and then acted as if we had a conspiracy of silence against her. Once in those days I had a strange thought when I looked at Kerrin.—I thought that if I could look like her and know that nothing could ever change it—not sickness nor fear nor accident nor age, nor anything—that I should not care very much what happened, that nothing would worry me any more. Kerrin was beautiful in a dark, odd way, and made with a brown cold skin tight-stretched, and wild colty eyes. She would stand sometimes turning her face before the mirror, or spread her hands out through her hair that was more like a thick red light than anything real. She'd crane and stretch her neck to see how the light looked smooth and syrupy over her cheeks, and it seemed sort of sad to me at times that all her loveliness was going to waste on just us, with none but a few shy stumbling fellows to see her, or farmers already married.

I felt little and mean in envying her and in wanting a beauty that nothing could ever change. I could not acknowledge it even to myself, but it was so. I used to wonder how men who had murdered or done crude and slimy things could go on living with the self which had made them do it still inside like a worm or ulcer; but now I could see how simple it was to make excuses.—How amazingly kind and tolerant we are to ourselves! What infinite patience we have!

I went and looked at my face in the glass. There was something wrong and dull in the lines of it. A pale smear with no life in the skin, and a mouth like a cut across. I was plain—O God, so plain! But still I had seen homelier people than I, and not minded them so much—loved some, in fact. I tried to console myself with this, but remembered that they had *strong* faces, though. We—I—seemed like a disease on earth compared with the other things. Our lives, buildings, our thoughts even, a sort of sickness that earth endured. These were grotesque and morbid broodings, but they came back often in the unbearable cleanness of this spring.

There were other things, though, more in the mind than these which the coming of Grant had brought, and sometimes even the scratch of Kerrin's return was forgotten in the sight of green elms and the ghost-green of new sycamore leaves. The poplar catkins opened down from the top branches first, and looked like red squirrel-tails swinging. The top sheaths fell while the lower branches were still in bud, and their wax-yellow beaks lay on the grass. I wished we could live on the sight of these things (it would be a lot cheaper, Merle said), but they were only a part and could not satisfy everyone. Most people have the blindness of new-born things—a not-incurable blindness, the sight being there but its use not known. But to Merle and me, even when we had first come, it seemed that our hearts must be small and shriveled-up things since they felt so tight and full with only an eye's breadth of loveliness to hold, and we wondered if they would grow or burst by the year's end, what with having to hold all the nights and days and seasons, the change from hour to hour, and the change from minute to minute even, from cloud-shadows moving up and down the hills.

In those early years, to read and to eat and to be alive on the hills had been enough for Merle and me. From the beginning we had felt rooted and born here, like the twin scrub-oak trees that grew together in the north pasture and turned lacquer-red in fall, and whose roots were under the white ledgestones. We called them the Gemini, and their inner branches grew short and were locked together so that the shape of both made only one tree with two boles.

At no hour did life suddenly change, nor was there any moment which could be said to have altogether made or altered us. We were the slow accretion of the days, built up, like the coral islands, of innumerable things.—The moment of evening air between the stove and the well outside . . . the sound of wind wrenching and whining in the sashes . . . the flesh of corn-kernels . . . fear—fear of the lantern's shadow . . . fear of the mortgage . . . cold milk and the sour red beets . . . the green beans and the corn bread crumbling in our mouths . . . fear again . . . and the voice of Kerrin singing to herself in the calf lot . . . the sense of safety in Mother's nearness . . . the calm faith that was in her and came out of her like a warmth around . . . the presence of each other and a lusty love of being, of living and knowing there was tomorrow and God knows how many more tomorrows and each a life and sufficient in itself. . . . We were added to by the shadow of leaves, and by the leaf itself . . . by the blue undulations across the snow, and the kingfisher's rattling scream even when creeks were frozen over. We were the green peas, hard and swollen, which Merle gathered late so that what was earth in the morning would be gone into and swelling out the peas by night, making them bigger all through no trouble or expense of ours, which seemed an odd, almost too kind thing—like a miracle when none was asked. They were as much part of us as the sight of white-boned sycamores flung up against the sky, or clouds driven like steam along the tops. In the thought and the strangeness of self we could spend hours as traveling through a labyrinth, and it was a riddle sufficient in those days to keep the mind quick and seeking, hungry and never fed; and in the mystery of the turnip, you forgot the turnip-leaf.

But for Kerrin these things had never been satisfying enough, even in other years. She used to get restless and savage, and rode out long ways into the night while we sat reading. "Where's Kerrin?" Father would keep on asking, would read a chapter and go peer out into the moonlight. "Why don't you keep her home, Willa?" he'd say to Mother. "How do you know what she's doing out this way? No girl ought to be out at night this way!" He'd be tired by dark, wanting to sleep early, wanted to go to bed by eight sometimes but insisted on staying up till Kerrin came back along the road, sometimes as late as nine or ten. We'd hear the plough-horses whinny and go thundering down the fence, and then the sorrel's feet rattle the road stones a fourth of a mile away, and hear his shrill, exhausted neighing. "She's here now," Mother would say. "She's safe enough. You go to sleep now, Arnold." And with the nearer rattling of stones and feet, Father would close his book, for a half-hour now unread, and go upstairs, having learned that he could not meet or say anything to her, and remembering the one night when she first had stayed this late and he had gone storming out to meet her, shouting for explanations he never got, and made inarticulate with rage when she would not answer or come into the house. She had spent the night out in the barn that time, sleeping up in the weedy hay and more comfortable perhaps than we were, sick and unsleeping in our beds.

I remember the morning after that night.—It was April, and cold, walled in with mists high as the sheep-barn roof. We saw Kerrin come out of the barn with dry scraps of weed still stuck in her hair, and stretch and yawn in the sun that came down through the mists, then come up the stones to the kitchen when Dad had gone. We looked at each other and shivered, but thought it was because of the fog that clung to our clothes and made them damp and chilly. We came down into the kitchen and flapped their dampness in front of the fire, and Kerrin sat at the table without saying anything, and the hay still messed in her hair. Her legs were wet and goose-fleshed from walking up in the grass. She watched us to see what we would say, but we only went on drying our clothes, more interested in the thick bacon smell and the glunk of oatmeal on the stove. Mother brought her some bacon and a hunk of toast and milk that had cream still marbled on the top, and told her she'd better move up against the stove to dry; and we could see she was hoping that Father would stay out a good long time. Kerrin ate savage and hugely like a wolf, and smeared on jelly till all her toast was gone, then ate the jelly plain in high, quivering spoonsful from the jar. Merle and I sat there and ate patiently at our blobs of oatmeal with milk around the edges. It came to me as a sort of dim, unfinished thought that there were hours of sun and hours of picking and hot hours on a stove all gone into those few minutes of Kerrin's swallowing and would become part of her, giving her energy to hate and use loud words and tears; and I wondered how Mother's faith would answer that, for it seemed to make the pattern of things more distorted than before. I hadn't time to follow this thought to the end —which was well, perhaps, for there was no answer, at least none that I could have found—for Father came in just then and stood in the doorway looking at us.

He was a big man and heavy, and his face hung dragged in long thin folds. His red hair used to be thick, but was now sparse and grown in somber hummocks. Once he had let it grow down over his collar, which made him look like a preacher and more kindly, but most of the time he was shaved and alien-looking to the earth. He had frosty eyes—a kind of white-blue with fierce pupils. I loved him sometimes when he smiled; because he so seldom did, I guess. He cared most for Merle and me, partly because we loved the land more, which seemed to justify and comfort him in a way. Merle he loved most, and used to say that she would have made a good boy. But he did not try to treat her as one, thinking that nothing could change a girl much. He looked at us from across the misty gulf that he thought was between him and all women, and thought of the place in which they moved around and did things as a long way off—a place from which they might step across this gulf to marry a man, but any time might go back again. Only Mother he saw clearly. The outside part of her anyway. If she went back in secret to this woman-place he did not know it, because marriage was to her a thing of which mighty few men are worthy—a religion and long giving.

He seemed not to see or to have forgotten Kerrin, might not have noticed her at all if she'd kept still and combed her hair instead of leaving it strawed and weedy. "Max isn't coming up today," he said. "He's sick." He put the milk down slopping over the floor, and looked at Kerrin. He started to say something, but only got red and tight and turned around in a helpless, exasperated way. Mother asked him how much they had finished yesterday, and he said it wasn't a third of what still was waiting. Max was slow, he muttered, and worked at home, besides—worked too much. . . . The Rathmans were planting corn, too. . . . Could silage it, anyhow, if it didn't sell. . . .

"Why don't you grow something that nobody else has got?" Kerrin blurted out. "Something that'll bring us more money than just corn!"

"You want too much too fast," Father said. He was cold and quiet and sounded years away from her nagging voice. He spoke as though to a little dog that insisted on yapping, a little dog that he might kick soon.

I could see Mother watching him, screwed hard and tense, saying—be careful . . . be careful . . . don't look at her that way! . . . Not aloud, but with her eyes. She was praying inside, I knew. Aloud she said, in a sort of indifferent way, that he might try celery later on, that it was hard to raise, she knew, but none around here had it and it took more water than anyone else had the time or means to give.

"Who'll haul the water?" Dad asked. Less of a question than a sneer. He had the old look of tiredness on his face that came when we argued with him, that look of being harried and forced to fight back against things not worth the battle. A look of woman-tiredness.

"I can do it," Kerrin said. She looked excited and eager in a sudden flare "Go ahead," Father told her. "Go ahead and see what you can do!" He shoved back his chair and sat there laughing to himself. An unpleasant and meager sound, exasperated and turned in as if to some other man, invisible inside, who understood and pitied him He seldom swore aloud, thought it was wrong to do before his girls;—but all the blasphemy was there, bursting and turning sour inside.

Merle and I sneaked away and went out of the house. The mists were all risen and we could see down into the valley where the peaches were coming into bloom and flecked with skinny rose. They were sparse that year and thin-petaled, but the wild plums flowered in clouds. There was a lane of them back behind the barns, and we went there past the fresh dung-heaps steaming warm and the tall hogs that rooted in the mud. The old sow Clytemnestra stared at us dully with suspicion and muttered, and with her were nine hairy shoats, following where her great dugs trailed along the mud. The air came sweet and stale and full of a grassy smell. We felt that a hard, smothering weight was gone, and climbed the fence and started to run fast and blunderingly over the gopher field. We wanted to reach the woods and be hidden in it. Shut ourselves off in the sparse green shadows. The hollows were full of the wild thin pansies, blue as if frost or fog were laid there—acres, it seemed, and covering the ground thick as grass itself. We went up past the pond where already there were clusters of slimy eggs from the frogs and salamanders, transparent and round like a bunch of tapioca balls black-specked and stuck together. Merle picked up one in her hand but it slid away like a fat and slimy fish, and seemed almost to squirm. We waited and watched, but could find no frog swelled up to sing, and nothing that seemed alive but the whirling beetles that darted and left their streaks on water like the scratch of skates on ice. The white-oaks were in tassel then—but there is no way to tell of them. We only stood like a pair of stumps, and looked and thought that something would break inside, and we felt too stretched and heavy to hold much more. Then Merle went down on her knees in the grass and started to pull up the pansies, almost savagely and in great chunks. "There're so many," she said. "Nobody'ud miss them if I pulled a thousand!" And I pulled some, too, and it seemed to stop the hurt when you got your hands tight on them, even knowing that they would die. . . . We found a bat in the wild shadbushes, clung upside down like the body of some gigantic moth, and his gold-brown fur had a metal light. Glowed orange. We peered in the wild gooseberry bushes and saw the mayflies dance there like a dust of pollen, and under the crab-trees found the dead leaves move where something had burrowed a tunnel, but we could not see its face or know whether it might be mouse or mole. Then Merle said, "Look!" in a bursting whisper and pointed up at a black-oak, hollowed out with disease and carrying great swollen lumps of bark,—and I saw the cold stare of barred owl-faces. Young ones with stony eyes. I felt ready to burst with excitement, wanted to shout and yet was afraid to move: having hunted their nest since we first came, knowing it must be somewhere near and hearing the old ones call and hoot back and forth even in daylight and early evenings.

I thought I was full enough of happiness to last

for the rest of life, to cover forever after the things like that morning in the kitchen, the things that were warped and grew misshapen and made life seem like a nest of biting ants. And then it came to me as it did at times when the woods seemed all answer and healing and more than enough to live for, that maybe they wouldn't be always ours—that a drouth or a too-wet year or even a year over-good when everyone else had too much to sell—could snatch them away from us, and a scratch on a piece of paper could cancel a hundred acres and all our lives. And this same sick fear came up again like a sly and smothering hand.

"What's the matter?" Merle wanted to know; and I think she could see the thoughts as though written plain on my broad smooth face, because she stood there chewing a twig, and all the inside light was gone out of her own. Above the fog of redbud trees and the wild plum, and across the moving sun-shadows, the buzzards went drifting on huge wings or rose up reluctantly from the brush, their red necks raw and sore-looking. And there was this same thought tunneling in both our minds.

But only in mad people fear goes on constant night and day, wearing one ditch in the mind that all thoughts must travel in. And as we were sane then and normal as the smooth face of a plate, the fear and the forgetting of it were balanced one against the other, and we no more brooded on this than the young calves would. We saw that the shadows were small and dwarfed by noon, and we were suddenly hollow with a hunger that no fear could make us forget or any wild ginger satisfy; and Merle hoped there would be muffins—big ones with hard tops; and muffins were more important and more wanted than all the hills on earth.

10

THIS is not all behind us now, outgrown and cut away. It is of us and changed only in form. I like to pretend that the years alter and revalue, but begin to see that time does nothing but enlarge without mutation. You have a chance here—more than a chance, it is *thrust* upon you—to be alone and still. To look backward and forward and see with clarity. To see the years behind, the essential loneliness, and the likeness of one year to the next. The awful order of cause and effect. Root leading to stem and inevitable growth, and the same sap moving through tissue of different years, marked like the branches with inescapable scars of growth.

In the first years it had not been hard to forget, to go out and come back and to take things lightly, the shadows heavy but passed through and forgotten. But later it was never the same. The power of living in the moment, with the past days and the ones to come blotted out for a time, grew less in these ten years. Only Merle seemed in a way to keep an almost child-like pleasure in moments of happiness without thought of their end or their beginning. She had not changed much in the years. In her still this spring were two people parallel: the sound, sometimes acid sanity, lucid and healthy as her flesh; and with it this half-raw sensitiveness, a dark superstition and childish fear. She was so old and young as to be hard to understand, and yet curiously simple, too. She was honest as light itself and had what I've always wanted—courage to live by her beliefs. So much of our lives we go through edgewise, shield-carrying, half of our living a lie. In the moment of trial we keep back the two-edged truth and sheathe it again. I wish we were hard-mouthed, chary of praise, and all our lives saying only the things we think are so. In this way only can we have values or standards of any sort. Merle came near to this, not intentionally but by being *born* honest. She did not fight half-heartedly with faceless shadows, masked forms she was afraid to name, but knew things for what they were and twisted them apart. She seemed to deny in her living what I had always found true—that love and fear increase together with a precision almost mathematical: the greater the love then the greater fear is. Merle had hated the mortgage, but never feared it, even though loving the place as much, if not more, than I did. I thought that if ever we rid ourselves of the debt, it would be through her stubbornness and hate. It seemed that way in the spring at least. One liked to believe there was strength somewhere.

11

THEN on a cold dry day toward the middle of April, Grant came over. It was a day no different from the rest,—the earth green by then, crab-buds fiery red and the hawthorns opening out, but the ground was cracked with drouth, and things bent over in the effort of being born. I watched him come up the road, and Father went out to meet him. So little new ever happened in our lives that not even all that came after has blotched out his coming in my mind. There wasn't much else to think of then.

Grant was older than I had thought he would be, and seemed at first a cragged and strange-looking man. He was tall and thin and we found ourselves staring up at his face like children. When he spoke his voice had a kind sound, almost old, and his smile was quick and sudden. He was embarrassed, we could see, but I noticed he had a quiet way of standing, not stiff and awkward like most men ill at ease. "He was scared and wanting to go," Merle said afterward. "I could see him get red under all his tan." But to me he had seemed very calm and patient.

"I'm glad you've come, Mr. Koven," Mother said. She spoke stiffly as though he were minister or sheriff, but she smiled and a person could see she meant it.

"It's good to have somebody new around," Merle blurted out. "—*Anything* new."

Grant laughed then, a big hearty sound, and looked much younger. "You make it easy for me," he said. "I'm glad that anything's going to do."

Father didn't know what to say and pretended not to hear him, and I only moved my head like an awkward stick when he told my name. Kerrin was not around. She wanted to meet him some way that was different from ours, preferring to choose her own time and place.

"It's going to be a good year this time," Father said at last. It was what he always said when there seemed a need for words and none came. "It's time for a big-crop autumn, and there'll be more than even the lot of us can do."

"It's time, God knows," Grant answered. "We're tired of feeding out husks instead of corn."

"A person gets worn out heaving the shocks around to find any ears," Merle said. "And the ears aren't fit for much but cob-houses.—Black smut and corn-boils. We didn't dare look what we dumped to the steers. Just pretended that it was corn."

Grant grinned. " 'It's the *shape* of corn, anyway,' Dad used to tell his heifers, and after a while they began to believe it better."

"Stomachs must have shouted loud enough to cover up their eyes," Merle said. "And when you've got seven—"

"You come out to the barn now," Father put in. "It's late, and we got some work to do." It was always late with Father, even at four in the mornings; I think that his sleep was a race between dark and light, and he lay with his boots a hand away on the chair beside him.

"Dinner'll be pretty soon," Mother reminded him. She had planned a good meal because of Grant's coming, and knew that Father delayed sometimes, forgetting to come unless she went out and told him. He got hungry, and cross because he was hungry, but didn't think of the reason why.

"You're only new once," Merle said to Grant. "—Only worth opening peaches for once. You'd better eat all you can now!"

"Who's buying peaches?" Dad wanted to know. He got red and flushed with suspicion, but Mother only laughed.

"It's a last year's jar," she told him. "Peaches you picked yourself."

Dad was embarrassed and walked away, and I wondered what Grant was thinking, and if he would get used soon to this hourly wrangling or if he had known it himself before.

"It won't take peaches to bring me in at noon," Grant said. "Hog-greens taste good when you're hollow enough." He smiled at Mother and around at the rest of us very fast, and went out after Father.

"He'll eat a lot," Merle said. "I can tell by the length that's on him. We should never have planned to feed him here."

"This'll be a good year," Mother answered. "We'll have food enough to eat anyway. Food enough if nothing to wear. We'll fill him somehow." She looked worried, though, and I saw her go back and recount the jars, as if by doing it over often enough she could make them more.

"Enough to eat anyway" . . . food enough . . . the words kept nagging me with some memory of their own, though I'd heard them often enough for them to carry no meaning any longer. "You farmers have food . . . food at least. . . ." And then I remembered the man who had come here years ago, and the old terror came back—the fear of being cast out of even this last retreat.

He had come in the fall of the year we moved, and the mortgage was even then like a rock that we carried always in our minds. There was a bitterness in sowing and reaping, no matter how good the crop might be (and that first year it was heavy as the oak mast and rich as weeds) when all that it meant was the privilege of doing this over again and nothing to show but a little mark on paper. And there was the need, the awful longing, for some sort of permanence and surety; to feel that the land you ploughed and sowed and lurched over was your own and not gone out from under your feet by a cipher scratch. I used to think of it sometimes when the orchards started to bloom and changed from a greyness into white fur along the plum branches, and a rose light came in the peaches. And I used to think of it when the apricots began to redden, and you could look down from the hog-lot's edge into a valley full of white smoke, more like a gulf full of white spray, where the giant pear trees were. I'd scratch my nail along the post and I'd think—when somebody does like this on a scrap of paper, then all these things are gone, and a little scrawl is bigger than trees or valley. But the fear was worse and more heavy after the man had come.

It was October then and we were carrying out sour milk to the chickens that morning, I remember, and we stopped by the fence-edge and saw him coming up the road. He came on slowly past the stripped plum thickets and the white-oaks that were barren then, and kept looking around but not as though he were seeing much. We stood and watched him, dumb-looking as two shoats, I guess, half-braced to run, yet curious to stay. When he got near us and in the gate, we saw that he had two skinny sacks and one had a lump of something inside that kept bumping against his back. He was yellow and liver-spotted and looked as though newly come out of a cellar's dark.

"Where's your Dad gone to, girls?" he said. He had a tired and unpleasant voice.

I pointed back to the barn, and Merle stared. He had on an overcoat, but it was too short around the knees and tight and had a black velvet piece on the collar, like Dad used to wear a long time past. His nose was red and kept running, and he wiped it off on his sleeve. Father came out and asked what it was he wanted. Spoke to him as though he were already proved a thief and caught.

"Need any help?" the man wanted to know. "Any picking or digging you aren't done with yet?—something I could crate up and get what's left?" He pulled a couple of sweet potatoes out and showed them. They were dry and warped-looking with bad spots on, but pieces that you could eat. "Got these from the last place," he said. "Ain't much, are they? But take up room in the stummick—"

"What's the idea?" Father asked. "What're you tramping around here for?"

"You farmers have got food anyway," the man said. "I got a family. We have to eat."

I was afraid of him and felt sorry for him. He looked mangy and worm-eaten and not used to walking. I wanted to tell him not to talk so defiantly to Father, tell him his way of asking was all wrong. I could see Dad hardening, getting cold and steely. It was the sound the man had of blaming it all on something else—on life or men or maybe God—that was setting Father hard against him. It was blasphemy, Father thought, for this man to thrust blame of his hunger onto something else. I wanted to warn him but I couldn't. Only stood there staring, with milk slopped down along my shoes.

"I don't need any help here," Father said. "A farmer's as pinched as any man. We don't raise stuff for the fun of giving." He glared at the man—at what used to be a man anyway, but was now only the shard of something crumbled. Glared at him and said, "Go on—get out!" I think it was that he didn't want to see him there, standing shabby with his jaundiced skin and his nose all slimy, looking like he was sick from his soul clear out and reminding Father of what might have happened to him if there hadn't been land to save us, and reminding him, too, of what might happen still. The man swore at him and turned back down the lane, crept off like something that wasn't a person or an animal,—more like a sick and dirty fly.

"A lying loafer," Father said. He turned and went back in the barn.

"We should have given him something," Merle said, and I thought of all the dug potatoes and the carrots piled and withering. I was afraid of him, but I couldn't stand the blob of pity that was smothering in my throat. I couldn't stand to see him go off that way with the limp sack holding its two potatoes, rotten around the end. "We can cut across the field and get him on the road," I said. "We can stuff things in my sweater." Merle was scared. She was afraid he would steal or murder us, I guess. And so was I. We went back and crept down in the cellar and snatched some potatoes up. Merle had carrots and an apple. We climbed the fence and ran out across the field. It was muddy and worse than plugging through deep snow. Merle fell twice and got her face all smeared. She was crying, and lost her breath to call. We saw the man then, passing around where the road-turn was, talking and swearing to himself, and the wind-twitched overcoat pulled tight around what was left of him. "Mister!" I shouted; but he didn't hear me for its faintness, like the shout of a person in a dream. I was embarrassed and stood there panting, with potatoes still lumped underneath my arms. I couldn't for fear or shame have called again. And then he turned the corner and was gone off out of sight.

I had never forgotten his mean and shabby face, and the pity I'd felt for the man himself; and the fear of what he had stood for came back so sharply at times that it might have been only yesterday we watched him go off in the wind. "Lord God!" I said in a sort of prayer, without knowing I spoke aloud.

Merle turned her red face away from the boiling carrots. "What's the matter?" she asked, but seemed to know without being told. She shook the pot fiercely over the flame and slammed the lid. "Potatoes were bad that year. We didn't have much ourselves!" She said it defiantly, but not as any excuse that she believed; she knew it was only a worn old argument used for the sake of peace. Small things stayed deep and hurt her, but she was able easily to forget, and they did not sour her moments of happiness. I wished that I could shift as quickly too from one weather to the next, and not let old fears spread out and stain even the things I loved.

Merle opened a jar of corn, pulling the cover off reluctantly but excited. She had forgotten the man already, and sniffed at the corn's sweet smell with a big grin on her face. The kernels were gold still and swam in a milky fibre. "Fifteen ears and a half," she announced. "All for one little jar.—If I'd have put the worms in, too, they'd have filled it better. Big milky things and fat!" She tasted a spoonful and poured the rest in a pan. "He'd better appreciate them now. We're not going to open another soon."

"There aren't any more *to* open," I told her. "That's the last one."

"We don't get a new man every day," Mother put in fast. "And it had to be done some time." She looked excited at having a guest, and young. It was strange how little she'd changed those years, in spite of the planning and work and the disappointments. I think that it was because she took life slowly, and trusted in something a person could neither feel nor see, but knew.

"Not a new man every day, thank God!" Merle mumbled. "This pot won't fill him as high as his heel, let alone the rest. Men that high ought to learn to eat something cheaper, something a person could buy by the ton or sack, like cobs or hay. God should have been more stingy with his bones, but it's too late now."

12

. . . I LIKE to remember that noon. Kerrin did not come in and we felt, as always, more free and at ease without her. Even Father seemed less impatient and screwed with worry, and ate two of the pickled peaches, forgetting to ask how many were left. I saw him put a whole half of one on his bread, and grin at the sweet-sour taste. It wasn't that Grant was a man easy to know and given to making much fun, nor was he quick and loud like Merle. But things struck him new and differently and he knew how to make his tales come alive. He talked with Father over all the old arguments and theories that we knew too well to debate or even to hear any longer; and, sometimes agreeing, made Father feel that he had a man to support him now. Grant had a kind of dry humor, too, bitter at times but never with any malice or littleness. Later he came to answer Merle back in her own way, but not knowing us well then only laughed at the things she said.

I sat and watched while they talked, and twice Merle piled the corn on his plate for all of her grudging words. The sun came in warm in long streaks across the floor, and the giant geranium plants made a pattern across its gold. When we touched our glasses, white circles of light would move on the walls and ceiling, and the cut-glass dish with the peaches in it made a rainbow-bar on the cloth. The food was good, better than it had ever been before, and Mother had made a braided roll with raisins. I forgot to add up what the bought part must have cost, and was glad of the sugar and cinnamon crust. Grant took a long breath of the spicy smell and then shook his head.

"There're words for most things," he said, "but none that I know of for this. It's the nearest to heaven a man can expect this side of Jordan."

"It's the nearest we're most going to get on the other side either," Merle said. She broke him a piece hot still and yellow.

Grant took a big bite and finished the cake in three. "It's good," he told Mother, "but all the praise that comes out of a person's mouth oughtn't to mean as much as the food that goes in. Eating's more honest than any words!"

"Then Max must have been a shouting man," Merle said sourly. "He ate like a hog, and never spoke when a grunt would do."

"Women like words too much," Father said. He leaned back in his chair with the ghost of a grin. "They like to be told what a man would see for himself. A woman'd get fat on words alone."

"Around in August you'll wish that was true," Merle told him. "There'll be more words and less eating *then*." She jerked her head toward the fields we could see beyond the barn, and even now there was cold dust blowing out of the furrows.

"May ought to bring us a flood," Father said. "Quit

nagging and give it a chance to rain. Three years of drouth never come together, and I've got a good man to help me now!"

"Drink him a toast in water," Merle said. "That's the greatest thing you could honor with, these days."

Father picked up a glass and drank the toast, with one of his few and sudden smiles. Then shoved back his chair while we sat there surprised, hardly believing we'd seen him do it. "A good dinner, Willa," he said, then turned very quick toward Grant. "We're late. Have to go. We've wasted too much already."

Grant stood up then and straightened himself with a jerk. His shoulders were wide and a little bent like vulture wings, and his long arms stretched out thin. "Not wasted for me," he answered Father. "I could plough up a mountain now."

"*Mountains* are what they are, all right," Father mumbled. "Rock-boulders and stony mud. . . ."

But he looked almost eager instead of grim.

13

I CAME to wonder how we had gotten along alone

in the days before Grant had come. He roomed with us and ate all his meals here, too, going back to his father's land sometimes on Sundays. Father was proud of him then, and acted as though he himself were glorified by Grant's strength; seemed to feel some credit due him. Grant's was a kind of long, loose-armed power, and I wondered sometimes with Merle how he moved all his dangling knots and bones hard and together enough to accomplish the things he did. "He looks like a gaunt old long-limbed tree," she told me once. Dad was around and turned fast on her. "That ain't for you to say," he shouted. "Grant's a good-enough looking man—better-looking than most!" Merle said maybe he was right and as long as Grant did the work he could look like a post or anything else and it wouldn't matter to her. He was as good-faced as a man has a chance to be, she said, since they have no way of *seeming* more handsome, as women do. Father stared at her, but didn't seem quick to catch what she meant. He thought that because she smiled it must be all right and complimentary enough, and trusted her not to sneer.

"Men are all like each other," Merle said. "We'll find him no different than any other. They're like as ponds. Seem to think that just being born sets them apart as gods!"

She talked like this, not with malice but believing it till one day that first week when he came up at noon and found her washing. He came up walking tired and slow the way Dad did, but his face more alive. He never smiled much, but strong and warm when he did, and his whole face lighted up ("Turns on," Merle said). He'd been ploughing and looked half-starved and his shirt was doused in sweat. Merle was tired, too, her big booming voice getting less loud until her singing was like a croak, and she only jerked her head at him for notice. Grant sat down solid and heavy on the steps, the way Father does—as though he were sunk there forever. Merle twisted the towels out, then pulled up the shirts and flapped them over the edge so he could see they were his own.

Grant jerked himself up fast, came over and told her to let him do the rest. "I've got the time now," he said. "You let me finish up these old sacks." Merle stained red as rust and started to blurt out something rude.—"What's the matter?" she started to say. "—You in a rush for the food?"—but managed to smear it over. Grant pulled out three shirts at once and twisted them all together. Squashed the buttons in half. Then he slung them over the line and stood back grinning, red and embarrassed. They were dryer already than the one he had on his back. Merle sat down on the steps, sagged up against the post, and told him to pull out the overalls. She thought him a little mad, I guess, but hoped that he'd finish before the spell passed over. Grant wrenched out the rest and emptied the tubs, and she stared at him as if he were a strange dinosaur or ghoul. I could see her mind changing before my eyes, a hard core softening up. "You're better than most," she told him. "Maybe just being a man isn't all the excuse you need for living."

"It's a good enough one," Grant said. He looked at her and laughed, and then asked why she didn't go in and start cooking.

"You've worked for nothing," Merle told him, "if that's why you wanted to help. Marget's done everything already." She snapped it at him, but not either angry or believing what she said. And I saw Grant watching her when she went away,—a sort of pleased look on his tired face.

14

I WENT back up to the pasture with him that afternoon. I'd never have gone but that he had left the water-jug there and needed more, drinking nearly a gallon in one morning. "You come up and get it," he said. "Let Merle finish the dishes. She's had her rest." Then went out fast before she could slop the water at him. (Only I doubt that she would have now that the pond had shriveled so,—shrunk two feet even then.) We went up the creek-road and he talked to me as though he had really wanted me to come and not just as someone to bring the water back. He never spoke of himself except when I asked him things. He remembered coming that time for the horse when Merle met him out in the yard. She was red and stumpy, he said, and her hair was fuzzy behind. When she saw the horse she had marched right past him "as though I were air or nothing, and pumped him some water from the tank.—Then glared at me like a little bull. Thought maybe I'd steal it from him!" Grant laughed as at something he'd thought of often and grinned over to himself.—I liked to think of her coming back to his mind that way.

The wild cherries were in bloom. It was hot still, and ink-blotter clouds messed up the sky but brought no rain. The spring green was like green sunlight or green fire—something, anyway, more lovely than just leaves—and there were yellow clouds of sassafras along the pasture. We found a snake in the hollow limb of a sycamore, peered close and saw that his eyes were like milk-blue stones, hard and round and without any pupils. I thought he must be blind, but Grant said that for a wild thing to be blind was death, and that it was only the old skin thickened over his eyes before he shed. I felt ashamed to have seen things like this year after year and never stopped to find out the reason or know more about them. Because there had seemed always time ahead, I guess, and never time then. Grant seldom let anything go past without trying to find the meaning of it. "I've got a fool hopeless belief," he said, "that the more we know the more we'll be able to understand."

"Maybe for you," I told him, "but for me only more confusion."

"Better to be confused than blind," he said. We

watched the snake gliding back, and his coils made a dry and scratching sound. Grant said that the scales would split off from his eyes first. "New eyes first, and then a new skin all over—there's a text for you, Marget! Lord, I should have been a preacher like Dad!" He put one hand on the fence post and threw himself over the wires, easy as if he had hurled a stone. He frightened the team and they started off, jerking the plough out of the ruts and lurching against each other. Grant didn't shout or bellow. He turned quick and grinned at me, then started off in a lumbering run. The horses got hooked up in the lines and didn't go far, but plunged around when he tried to untangle their feet. He didn't come back when the mess was over, only waved and shouted out something about long-legged fools, which meant all three of them, I guess, and started off up the row singing louder and worse than Kerrin.

Coming back it occurred to me how Dad would have been if this had happened. Hot and howling and angry, not being able to keep things from making him seem ridiculous, and fearful of anything that might tip over his dignity, poor-balanced and easily overthrown. Grant's furrows were straighter than Dad's or

Max's ever were. He ploughed deeper, too, and it made me believe that seed might get underground before winter after all.

15

THAT month was unreal and beautiful. No rain came, but it did not seem to matter much. I did not care any more. I forgot the mortgage and the payment due next month, forgot there was anything to fear, and lived in a sort of fog of nameless happiness, indefinable and seeming to have no source, like the spring smell that comes in March before there is even a shred of leaf or flower. I was happy without excuse or reason. The pear trees seemed more beautiful than in all other years, with a strong musk-sweetness on the wind. But even spring was only a lesser miracle. I think now—almost unbelieving—of those first few weeks, remembering the blind happiness that not even the worry over Kerrin could change. Father was for a while more cheerful too, having someone besides just us to talk to now, and someone who felt as he did; although the rest of us could see from the beginning that they were acres apart in thought, and Grant ahead in a hundred ways. Grant liked our father, liked him so much that he never or seldom would show him up before us, though he could have done it whenever we talked together. And only when they were alone would he cancel out arguments, sometimes in a single line or word, with facts that Father either had overlooked or more often not known about. I'd overhear them sometimes and marvel, not so much at all that Grant knew and his way of seeing things whole, as at his power of toppling Dad's pyramids of thought so that the crash was plain enough and yet without angering him. And Dad thought of Grant as one a little radical and free-thinking perhaps, but a man with sound reason for everything that he had to say.

Grant was a much kinder man and less hard than his own beliefs—beliefs that had grown out of acrid and salty experiences—but there was a layer of stoniness inside him. Some people are soft like quagmire: you touch, and touch down in farther, fumble and press in an ooze of uncertainty, not finding a shard of flint anywhere. But in Grant there was something solid, not arrogance, but a bed-rock of belief. It wasn't belief in divine goodness, either, but something that served him better. To trust so much in anything—

even in one's own sight—may be a form of blindness itself; but there is a driving force in blindness. It's the only way to achieve anything, I guess: to put great blinkers on the mind and see only the road ahead.

That he should have this hard, almost cynical attitude toward things and yet at the same time so much kindness, made me feel a gratitude nearly pain. I remember the thankfulness I'd have whenever Dad got his history mixed and tried to prove points before us at the table, and Grant would let it go by, knowing the answer but not wanting to make him seem ridiculous and lay him open to Kerrin's spite.

Grant had liked Kerrin then. It was not hard to understand, and perhaps I might have, too, had I been he. Might even have loved those things that I hated in her—her fierce unexpectedness and shifting, even her selfishness. . . . She didn't come in for supper at all any more; and I'd thought it strange at first, since Grant ate here every night, but began after a while to understand—if Kerrin is ever to be understood. It was a part of her difference from us, and partly a desire not to take or to meet him in the same way that we were doing—as one of us. She realized, too, in a sort of distorted way, his clear seeing of things and that he would not always excuse the restless and clever cruelty in her that attracted him sometimes. . . . I wanted to forget her, wanted to pretend a little longer that tomorrow—some time—she would be different. Or gone. It seemed at times that this feeling of waiting, of life suspended and held in a narrow circle, would go with her. I knew that this wasn't so, that nothing would really begin that had not its roots in ourselves, but could not help feeling she was the thing that caused this smothering. There was something in her—or lacking—that kept her from seeing outside the warped and enormous "I." It came to me that she would do anything she chose, because she saw wrongly and did not need any excuse but desire. . . . What is sanity, after all, except the *control* of madness? But it must be something more, too, a positive thing,—inclusion of love and detachment from self. . . . I had to fight up thought by thought to things known and recognized all my life, and yet until this year never realized.

But until May the first fog of happiness covered up much of this, and stood between me and the real seeing.

16

MAY was a queer month. The beginning of understanding. A cold dry month. Rot-sweet smell of mandrakes on the air, but most things almost too chilled to bloom. No rain, and dust coming up behind the plough. Cold dust is a sort of ominous thing, and Father began to worry over the shrunken pond. These things were sourly appropriate to the month's end, and yet it began with a quiet ecstasy and happiness.

I went over to the Rathmans' on the first of the month for seed. Max had a new car by then, out of his wages from the road, but not paid for as yet. He got to town more often than Father did, and brought us back stuff from Union, but said our land was too rutted to drive his car along and so left what he bought down at his house,—a thing which was like Max to do, and we took it for granted now. I was glad to have reason for going there, though. They seemed so solid and safe, and needed so little. Old Rathman had a good market for his grapes, and made wine with what was left over. He knew where to sell, and trucked his stuff to the doors. Their land was their own entirely and had no debt. Whatever grew on it belonged to them and went to pay back no unseen owner and the garden shoved up to the edge of the door, kohlrabis undermining the steps almost. Everything old and rich like the earth.

Theirs was more sheltered land than ours, flat and set in the footsteps of a hill. Old Rathman had not been off the place for ten years, but Karl had gone off to Bailey and married there, and Max got his job on the road. Only Aaron was left of the three to help him. I think the old man had been glad to show them he managed as well alone. He never rested, and looked like a warped old gnome with his hat on top.

This day he was not so sure of himself, but still not fearful. "Two acres of strawberries shrivel up like leafs do," he said. "Hard . . . dry. . . . No rain! Is one to water by hand? *Nein! Let* them shrink up!—the Gottdamn little measles!" He grinned then and picked me some from the crate-toppings. All his berries were big on top, and the wizened ones underneath. "Give her a crate, old lady," he told Mrs. Rathman, and pointed his hand at the flabby spinach leaves. "We can't eat all of dem tinks." I tried to tell him we had an acre of *dem tinks* wilting over at home, but he wouldn't listen.

Old Mrs. Rathman was hungry to talk, herself, and told me about the sweet potatoes that Max had raised special for just himself last fall but didn't recognize when she got them cooked. She told me about this Lena Hone who was Max's girl . . . "nice as cream in her way of talking . . . black eyes and hair . . . not much to look at though . . . reminds me of you in a way. . . ." She hoped Max would marry soon and stay to home. That Mary of Karl's hadn't no children yet. Maybe Max would have better luck with Lena. Would I stay longer? No? Well, a jar of apple-butter then . . .

She must have been beautiful once; her hair white now but her polished eyes unchanged and a kind of grave humor wrinkling her cheeks. I wondered what it was like to live safe. Out of debt. I could not believe that they had their own rawness, too, something gone bad under all this white-looking comfort. And there *was* nothing then.

Old Rathman stopped me before I left and asked about Grant. "Vot does Pop tink about his new fellow? Better than Max was, maybe?"

I told him that Grant was pretty good, and then he wanted to know if I knew about Ramsey's loan. Did

I know that "this colored man Ramsey" (Rathman always spoke of him in this way, not with hate or suspicion, but as of a creature from some other earth, as one might speak of a Bushman or giraffe) —did I know that this fellow was almost drove off his place last year? I said no, and he told me that Ramsey had come to him and asked for money to pay his rent. " 'But I ain't got any money,' I told him. 'I got land and vegetables, but no money!'—Maybe I should have give him kohlrappys to pay his rent! The old lady give him a jar of pickles but no money."

Then I made out from his rambling words that Ramsey had gone to Kovens' and gotten the money there. Rathman knew because he had asked old Koven himself. At first Grant had told Ramsey not to pay—too big a rent anyway. "Let'm try to shove you off and see what'll happen," he'd said. Christian was scared, though, and not willing to risk it. "Maybe you could get by all right," he told Grant,—"you ain't a nigger. You don't have a wife and seven children. A nigger can't wait and see what'll happen. He *knows!*"

Grant had loaned him the money then, and would have given it sooner but he hated to pay off Turner who didn't need it and who'd dangled the debt over

Christian's head until he was raw as a negro could get. To pay off Turner had seemed to Grant like throwing his money down in a sink or propping a wormed old shed with good new poles, but better at least than having the roof crash down on Ramsey's head. You couldn't stand by and do nothing just because you thought it was wrong for a man to be trapped that way.

"Gran' won't be loaning no more, I guess," Rathman said. "Koven's two years behind in his taxes now."

Here were all of us then, I thought, crawling along the ruts and shoving our debts ahead like the ball of dung-beetles. Worse off than the beetles themselves who can bury their load and be done.—All of us but the Rathmans, anyway. They're safe, I thought, padded in from fear. They have only to work for the now, and not pay for the years behind. . . .

I came back through their orchard where the early apple trees were in bloom, thick as a snowstorm with white flowers, and the branches long-curved and reaching to the ground. Dear God, but they were beautiful! I stood a few minutes under one that was like the inside of a great white bowl. Chickadees pecked at the scaly bark for aphis and kept up a crying clack. I felt light and foolishly happy,—the Ramseys, the mortgage and Kerrin forgotten and only shadows. And I knew it was partly the hot flower-smell, but more because we had talked of Grant and I'd heard his name.

17

BY THE middle of May nearly all of last year's cans were gone. Nine jars spoiled. Mother spoke as if this were her own fault for some reason, not blaming the cheap jar-rings that Father bought. He had to, I guess, since there were new dairy sterilizers to buy, and tried to cut down on the things that we used for ourselves. The jars had a rancid and stomach-filling smell that stayed on the hands for hours after we threw the stuff away. The cows gave less milk, and six gallons were lost because of the onions. Milk was scarcer everywhere, but we didn't get much more at the dairy than before. Last year there had been too much, and all farmers had it; Father got less for the gallon on account of Rathman's sending his cans in, too. This year nobody had very much, but the price didn't seem to change—not at the *back* door of the dairy anyway. There was a wry perfection about the way things worked.

I wished to God it would rain. I could walk in the stream beds by the quarry, and only the ghostly plantain grew stubbornly in the fields. The ground was cracked wide open and Dad was beginning to get more desperate, seeing the pastures start to yellow already. . . . These things are not hard to tell of now. We were used to them and we still had hope. But the things we felt most are hardest to put in words. Hate is always easier to speak of than love. How shall I make love go through the sieve of words and come out something besides a pulp?

Grant was kind, very kind to me. I could not have asked for anything worse. Something snatched and blundered inside me when I heard his voice unexpectedly, but after a while the foolish ecstasy and fog dried up, and there was only the pain and the reality left. I came to see more clearly after one night when Grant and I had gone up to the north pasture together, hunting his watch that he'd lost near the plough. The stars were windy and brilliant, and one enormous planet burned down along the west. It was dark with no moon, but the white patches of everlasting gleamed out disk-like in the grass. "You hunt near the plough," he said, "and I'll thrash in the weeds where it might have jumped." Then I found it half-buried down near the plough nose and deep in a dusty furrow. The watch was an old big silver thing, and one that he'd owned for years. Grant never could tell the time by sun nor tell it by being hungry. "I'd be coming back in for supper while Merle was wiping up breakfast still," he said. "Don't trust anything natural, Marget. —Only the little wheels." He looked at its round dull gleam in the starlight, and wiped off the dust from its face.

There was a fierce sweet smell from the crab-trees, and I peered up at the stars through their twisted branches. Everything drops away, comes to be unimportant in the dark. It's like sleep almost. A freedom from self, from ugliness,—escape even from thought of Kerrin and debt and tomorrow. Dark's like the presence of a father confessor.—Now lay down all the scrabble of your lives . . . confess all the phantoms . . . unburden yourself in dark of the day's accretions. . . . But when I said to Grant that night was the one sure healing which nothing could steal from a person, he shook his head. "No healing for me, Marget. Night is a sort of blindness. A thing to be gotten over with. I like noon. Short shadows. Like to see what I'm doing." "—Sun'll not always show you that," I wanted to say. But didn't. Grant had no flat drab face to hide. Nothing that wouldn't bear noon sun on it. What was it to him that Kerrin got more irrational all the time? What was our mortgage to him? . . . This sense of impermanence and waiting? . . . Love's unintentional hate?—*He* could go when he wanted to. *He* didn't feel any need for safety and solid earth. Nor did the awful waste in life bother him. There was this layer of hardness in him that accepted things without breaking. . . . I was quiet, thinking these things, and we came back soon. There was no reason to have stayed, but it seemed almost a sin to sleep those nights, blind and dead to the stars. We were so tired, though, that they didn't matter. Father and Grant used to sleep like clods of iron, and Merle wouldn't have waked if God Himself had waited outside in the night. But Kerrin went out after dark more than she ever used to.

She was gone still when we came back in, but Father thought it was she in the door with Grant, and turned toward us, trying to see in the smoky light. "Where've you been, you two?" he shouted. The lamp shook in his hand, casting out shadows like black fire, and made his glasses gleam out. Grant understood Father pretty well and knew how to calm him down, or at least not make things worse. He told him we'd been out hunting his watch. "Marget found it down in a rut," he said. "I think she can see in the dark." Then Father saw it was I and not Kerrin, and made a sort of relieved, embarrassed grunt. "That you, Marget?" he asked. "You'd better come up to bed soon." He went upstairs then and left us standing together in the dark. It was I and not Kerrin, and so there was nothing to fear or shout over.

I saw quite plainly what he had meant; nor did it hurt less to know that this was true.

18

. . . I BEGAN to see clearly what I had already known, and yet had not gone far enough in thought to face. I think I first knew it plainly not through any word spoken, but from watching Grant's face at times when it wasn't guarded. Grant wasn't a simple man like Father. Not one with his love and hate near his eyes or mouth. I liked it in him and yet was confused, not being used to people who, like myself, kept their feeling so much hidden.

What Merle felt then, I do not know. We never talked direct or openly of him except in an ordinary way. She spoke sometimes in a brief, almost pitying scorn of the way Kerrin was, and laughed at her sometimes without malice and as only a person neither hating nor loving could. . . . We'd see them standing together over the snake-fern Grant had dug up for Mother, which Kerrin would go out and water every day at the time when he came up with the milk; and Merle would look at me and smile. We'd hear her shrill black laugh, and see Grant smiling down at her hot excited face. I was glad when the fern died and we didn't have to see Kerrin going through with her farce of caring about it every night. It's hard to watch people acting fools. (Harder still to watch her dumping out quarts of water on the fern.) Grant tried in sort of pathetic ways to please, and had dug it up out of the ravine woods. When it died we didn't tell him, but Merle did. She pointed out the dry shriveled thing and said something of "early hay." Grant laughed but turned red as brass. He went out to dig up another, but couldn't find any more. "Why does he have to be always pulling things up and moving stuff?" Merle asked me. "Why can't he leave them alone to grow where they started? Enough things dying without his help!"

In other ways, too, Kerrin was the same.—She had used to take water out twice in the mornings when they cut the hay. I offered once, because she looked tired and I thought she might want me to take it for a change, but she turned on me like a mountain-cat and almost shouted. "You never used to," she said.—"What do you want to now for?" Looked at me hard and burst out laughing. . . . There was no use to hate. I told myself this: We have no time to hate; it's a blind, terrible waste—but I could not help it. . . . Kerrin wanted Grant, wanted him more than anything else she had ever snatched at. Because he was tangible, I suppose. It wasn't the real Grant that she wanted or cared about, because she had never known him underneath. She made me think of the carrion vines that move with a hungry aimlessness, groping blindly in all directions till they find a stalk to wrap on.

I let her go then—she wasn't much good for other work anyway—and went on down to the strawberry patch. The sun was hot like a blanket of fire across the shoulders, but the wind cold. The ground cracked open and overgrown with crowfoot. The patch was an old one and had few berries. They were hard to keep up each year and replant all the time. I was tired, but the grass smelled good—a hay smell, yet full of green. I remembered years ago sitting down on a ledge of stone under a buckeye tree, and its yellow flowers sifting down like a rain on the ant hills underneath. I don't know why this should have come back now, except that I remembered how good it had felt to do nothing then and sit there resting my puffed-up feet, not caring or worrying over anything else. I'd been tired, but it wasn't the same as the feeling this spring: not the tiredness of long waiting and doing things month after month with no change. Nor was there the weight of all these things—I wished I were ten years younger, or ten older! If I were younger, they would not exist; and older—I could learn to accept them. I wished there were someone I could tell all this to. If it had been told, it would not have weighed me down so much. But I could not tell anyone here and go on living with them, knowing they knew and were thinking about it, staring at me with this in their minds. They would have been kind, I know, but kindness is sour comfort.

PART TWO THE LONG DROUTH

BY JUNE things were shriveling brown, but not everything dried and ugly yet. It was not so much the heat and dryness then as the fear of what they *would* do. I could imagine a kind of awful fascination in the very continuousness of this drouth, a wry perfection in its slow murder of all things. We might have marveled and exclaimed and said there was never anything like it, never anything worse, and shaken our heads, recalling all other years in comparison with a kind of gloomy joy. But this was only for those to whom it was like a play, something that could be forgotten as soon as it was over. For us there was no final and blessed curtain—unless it was death. This was too real.

But sometimes, even in this year, the beauty of certain hours and places was so intolerable that it contracted the heart and left me without words. There was an unearthly smell in evenings, a strange mingling of wild grape and catalpa sweetness with honeysuckle come to flower and unknown blossoming things, and I woke up at night to blinding moonlight and the complaining of a catbird in the firebushes. The black marsh-fields swarmed with fireflies that seemed to stand still in the air for seconds at a time. The earth was overwhelmed with beauty and indifferent to it, and I went with a heart ready to crack for its unbearable loveliness.

For Merle there was a sort of glory in all things, a haloed way of seeing them—I do not know how to tell it—not only in the peacock-blue and brown skins of the lizards, or in the obvious and almost blinding whiteness of the daisy fields, but in everything she saw or did.—In the stoning of cherries and the acid stain in her skin, and the heat and confusion of their preserving . . . the stove raging and too hot to come near, and the steam from the boiling glasses . . . the cherries dissolving in a rich syrup-redness. . . . She stormed around among the kettles, tasting and slopping,—shouted Whoa! and Haw! to the cherries pouring over, dripped wax with one hand and stirred with the other, and sniffed at the strong smell of burned juice blackening where the stuff boiled over. I don't know what it was—only health perhaps, too much to be contained inside and radiating out like her overstoked ovens. And then again she'd be quiet, shaken down to dumbness at the sight of wheat fields, red-orange and clean like blown fur over hundreds of acres.

The cherries were thick this year in spite of drouth, and Grant brought the fruit up when she didn't have time; even stoned cherries for her in the evenings, and stayed up late when she canned at night. He did it because he liked pies, he said, and was fearful that Merle would fall asleep and put away God knows what in the jars. The smell of boiling cherries was sweet enough, with a good and acid tang, but I kept thinking of how the sugar was getting down, and wished that Merle would put less in and see if they'd keep that way. I wondered what good all the fruit was going to do us if we couldn't pay for even the jar-rings soon. There were too many for us to use, but not enough to market since we hadn't enough to ship and the Union markets were overflooded. It hurt to see anything wasted, and sometimes we trucked them along with the milk.

"Give them away," Mother said. "Better than swelling the jays and worms. Somebody'll take them if it don't cost."

"We won't waste spray on the things next year,"

Father mumbled. "A man can't afford to give when nobody gives him back. You can't work without profit when nobody round you does. I'd give for no cost if I could get back for nothing."

"Somebody's got to begin," Grant said.—The only time that I've ever heard him try to stir Dad into useless anger.

"Not just somebody!" Father shouted. "Not just me or you or us!—Everyone's got to do it. It ain't possible to give away milk and hogs and time when you have to pay plough and oil—and a man to help!"

"It's about what you're doing, anyway," Grant said.

Father pounded his fist on the table. "Maybe that's so," he snapped, "—maybe so, but I ain't going to call it right!"

I listened and thought I had heard this a thousand times. It was as new and old and stale and important as the weather.

Then Father had turned to me, glad for excuse of changing the talk, and told me to go up to Ramsey's that night and ask if he'd loan his mule tomorrow, and that if he would we'd give him help cutting corn in September. Grant looked at Father as though he wondered where we would find the time, and so did I. I wondered, too, if Christian would loan his mule for nothing.

"Maybe you won't have time in September," Kerrin said. "We've got our own corn to cut."

"Dad'll make time," Mother spoke up fast. "He's done it before.—Ramsey planted more corn than we did. He's going to need the help."

"I can't work a galled horse," Father said to Kerrin. "I got to have one of Ramsey's mules. Who's going to *pay* to rent 'm?" He looked at her hard and waited.

She backed down then and told him to go ahead. "Go on," she said. "—You'll be sorry."

Dad grinned in a sort of helpless, exasperated way and turned at me again. "You go," he said. "Merle'd take too long—she talks too much. You won't waste time like she does."

"Lucia'll talk just as much to Marget;—she'd talk to a fence post even," I heard Kerrin say, not loud, but intending me to hear,—and I went out fast so it would seem that I couldn't have heard her.

It was getting dark by then and Grant saddled the horse for me. "Ramsey'll loan the mule," he said. "Don't let Lucia give you their whole farm too."

2

I RODE the three miles thinking a good deal of Grant, and did not notice whether or not they seemed long. There was a kind of painful pleasure in thinking about his face—the gaunt nose and his plain eyes that saw a lot more than Father or even than Merle did. I saw him standing stooped over the boiling cherries, tasting to please her—and himself as much, his big hands holding the spoon like a spade; and Merle with her face a furious red from the steam, making her eyes a sudden unnatural blue, glaring at him with a dare to criticize, and great bursts of laughter at seeing his puckered, grimacing mouth. It seemed strange to me that she did not realize what was written all through and over him,—and strange that she did not love him anyway. I did not want to see Merle humble with love for any man, but I wished she could give him something more than this casual caring, and feel more than a need for someone to tilt against. He might just as well have been one of us and lived here years for all that he seemed to make her feel. I wished she could see and give back something, and hated to think that Grant might suffer sometime the way I had—and still did at times. . . . I have one thing at least to be thankful for out of all the petty and swarming thoughts: I have never been jealous of Merle, never prayed that Grant would not care about her; have even tried to make her understand him better sometimes. This is not much, but it is a little anyway.

I rode in the strange mixed smell of hay and darkness, weeds and the cattle lots, and farther on the heavy malt smell of the oat fields down near Ramsey's. I thought to myself—if anything could fortify me against whatever was to come (and there were times when, in spite of an everlasting hope, I felt we were moving toward some awful and final thing), it would have to be the small and eternal things—the whip-poor-wills' long liquid howling near the cave . . . the shape of young mules against the ridge, moving lighter than bucks across the pasture . . . things like the chorus of cicadas, and the ponds stained red in evenings. . . . As long as I can see, I thought, I shall never go utterly starved or thirsty, or want to die . . . and I thought this because I did not know, because I still had hope that Grant was not beyond me, and because I could still see him and hear him at least. I was afraid, though, and prayed.—Lord make me satisfied with small things. Make me content to live on the outside of life. God make me love the rind! . . .

There was a light at Ramsey's, and I heard Ned hollering: "G'wan!—g'wan—let me up! Get yoh butts outa ma face, Chahley," and I heard their wild savage singing and Lucia's laugh. No sound from Christian, though. "A deep-taking man," Lucia says. And a rare one, a negro quiet almost to dumbness, loving land more than company.

Lucia hoisted herself up and lighted a candle, and the children came up cautiously, shy and giggling to each other. They made faces and ran away shrieking, except Henry who stood and stared, half-hidden behind Lucia's enormous arm. "Henry's like Chrishun," Lucia said. "Follows him everywhere quiet."

"I hoed," Henry announced in a loud burst, and disappeared in an agony of shame behind her skirt. Christian sat hunched and tight in his chair, the candle making his face like a black carved skull, and a reflection of fire in the stained balls of his eyes. He brooded and seemed absorbed in something beyond us both, and Lucia did all the talking, her voice a deep and comforting boom.

There were two rooms in the house (one a sort of shed for the dogs and chickens), and around us the beds and sacking bulged dimly in the corners. There were a stove and table and the close, rich smell of air used and over-used and mixed with stale coffee and soup. The walls were covered with pictures: torn Bible illustrations—The Good Shepherd and The Widow's Mite—and advertisements for liver medicine. The corners were deep with old newspapers stacked up for the stove, and bundles of kindling salvaged on Christian's trips to town were chucked underneath. It was thick inside, and mosquitoes whined in and out of the torn screens, but Lucia rocked calmly and seemed unconscious of all their stings. Round silver balls of perspiration stood out on her face and dripped down her polished cheeks like placid tears.

For ten years Ramsey had rented land and expected to buy, but all that he ever did was make his rent-money and put up half the crop to go over the winter. In five years they saved fifty dollars and then had to spend it to get a new team. But every spring Lucia boomed out that *this* was the year they were going to make it. Ramsey'd mutter the same thing, too, and all that they ever did was pay the rent. . . . I told them I'd come for help and they looked surprised, and all of a sudden it occurred to me that we seemed to them as the Rathmans did to us. Safe. Comfortable. Giving appearance of richness, with our dairy and corn and chickens, our steers and team and orchard —although each thing was barely paying to keep itself. . . . I told them about the gall, and Lucia looked back at Christian, waiting for him to say. She'd have given us both the mules, herself, and everything else she could lay her hands on if I had asked her alone.

Christian stared down at his hands and answered slow, as if it were effort to talk. "You kin have them both," he said. "They don' pull good sepurate.—It don' matter about you helpin' in the fall."

"Chrishun don' think we'll be here to cut that corn," Lucia said. "We can't make any rent-payments ovah to Turner's. We got to pay him in cash and half the crop, and we ain't *got* any cash this yeah.—He ain't goin' to root us out, though! Ah'm goin' stick heah tight! Turner have to yank pretty hard to get *this* big black tick out of his ol' houn's ear!"

"Koven ain't goin' to lend us again," Christian mumbled. "They ain't got anything either now."

"Gran' Koven work for you folks now—that right?" Lucia asked me.

"Board and shares," I told her. "Father can't pay him much. Old Koven lives off their steers and savings. Enough for himself but nothing over."

"Gran' went to school," Lucia said, "and Mistah Koven's a minister. Gran's a good man."

I liked to sit there and talk to them about Grant, speak of the things I liked about him to someone who wouldn't suspect or find me out. "Grant works hard," I told her. "Harder than anyone that I ever knew, except my father. Seems to have a good time some, too. Reads at night. Never gets mad with heat like Dad does."

"Your Pop's a good man!" Christian burst out suddenly. He looked at me hard with his stained round eyes, and then sank back again into brooding.

"Chrishun don' like folks to talk about your Dad," Lucia said. "Most people he wouldn't let have his mules!"

She came to the door with me, her great body blotting the light behind, and snuffed the air. Then she looked at the stars, always too clear now, never changing or covered. "Might rain tomorrow," she said.

"—Don' feel like a frost anyway." The children giggled and Christian gave an exasperated laugh.—"Bettah get out your ark, Lucia," he said.

Lucia grinned. "Chrishun's got a bile-stomach," she said. "It makes all his words come out sour. You tell your Pop that he's welcome, only not to let 'm catch cold."

. . . It seemed a long way back. I was glad to get the mules, but uneasy with the obligation and afraid already that it would never be paid—having debt enough now, without adding the weight of kindness to it. I couldn't think of much else, though, but the relief of getting home and lying in bed asleep. Unsaddling the horse was effort to even think about, and I tried to smother the tiredness with pretending that Grant might wait up and do it for me. Then even this was set aside and there was only the horse's lurch and stumble, and the ache of tiredness like a stone on top of my lungs. The stars were foolish pin-points of pain, and I wondered whether I ought to use peas or spinach first, and how soon both would dry up anyway, and if Kerrin would remember—or do it if she did—to scrape out the chicken house, and how Dad would take it when he found that matches were gone up a cent and a half.

There was a light by the barn when I came back, and for a minute I thought that perhaps Grant had really waited, and my hands shook on the reins with a stupid hope. Then Merle came out of the oak-shadow and helped me to strip off the saddle, and took Cairn down to drink.

"Everybody's asleep," she told me, "—especially Grant. Didn't notice how grey the dishes were he wiped, or stop even to wash his face. Tired out as an old mule."

I asked if Kerrin had gone in yet, and Merle said she was sleeping, too. "Maybe we'll get some work out of her for a change," she said, but her voice didn't sound like her words.

"What'll we do with her?" I burst out at Merle. "She never is well any more—looks like the ghost of a person. It's awful to see her ruin herself this way! It's awful to see her so unhappy!"

"You can't do anything," Merle said. "She's always been that way. She doesn't belong here, and there's no place else for her to go.—She asked Grant to sing again tonight, but he fell asleep instead.—Slumped down like a dead person in his chair."

We went inside then and saw a light still burning in Kerrin's room, faint and uncertain like a candle, and looked at each other. The house was still and hot, and the mosquitoes came through the torn screen places, even where Merle had glued on paper. We went in and lay down, and Merle slept without moving, soundly as though she were still seven and consciousness only a shoe or pin, worn when needed and as easily put aside. But I lay awake a long time, wondering what would happen if no rain came pretty soon, and how Dad was going to meet his taxes. I remembered that this was June, and started to figure the value of all we owned; and if the new shed for the horses had been such a good thought after all, though Grant had built it for nothing, and the old one was rotting like oaks in swamp. I thought that maybe we should have waited until July and not added even ten cents to what the tax was already going to be. I remembered I had the cooking tomorrow, and wasted a long time figuring how to make up a cake without sugar that might taste like one that had;—and then Kerrin's light went out and I heard her move in bed, and the old haunting fear came back—a kind of dark stain over all other thoughts. We seemed to lie here locked and coffined inside ourselves, and only Merle still free of the love or hate or fear that was shut inside. And it seemed to me, lying there in the dark, that the more I thought or read or saw, the more oppressive and tangled with choice life came to be. Not tangled in daily living, perhaps, but in the whole plan and pattern of it. The living itself was easy enough to do when the days were too full for thought, and clothes wearing down fast to bone, soaking up dirt like sponges. There was no question of *what* to do when it took two hours to get food ready for fifteen minutes of eating, and no particular choice to make except between radishes and beans. But it was the meaning of all these evident things that still stayed hidden. Every new thought seemed to open a door, but when the mind rushed forward to enter, the door was slammed shut, leaving it dazed outside. I seemed often on the threshold of some important and clarifying light, some answer to more than the obvious things; and then it was shut away. There must be some reason, I thought, why we should go on year after year, with this lump of debt, scrailing earth down to stone, giving so much and with no return. There must be some reason why I was made quiet and homely and slow, and then given this stone of love to mumble. Love *was* a stone!

And suddenly I wished to God that Grant had never come here at all.

3

JUNE dragged on with a heavy heat. By seven the birds were still as at noon, and the sun was a weight of fire on the leaves. No rain came at all. Aphis killed most of the radishes, covered them over so thick that the leaves were hidden, and black ones stuck like lice on the lettuce-heads. So much died that I wondered where all the work came from still left to do.

There was talk of strikes, rumors of meetings in Carton and down near the river. And then the unrest crept nearer, spreading out like a slow tide over the farms around us, until even Father began to notice. Grant went to meetings at night up in the school, and came back excited but not certain. He tried to get Father to come and listen, but Dad always said he had no time. "You go," he'd say. "You can tell me about it. I ain't the time."

Then Grant told him one night he'd have to hold back the milk tomorrow, and Father was angry and confused. "Who says so?" he shouted. "Who's going to make me lose the little I got? What're we going to live on now?"

"On hope, I guess," Grant said. "A sacrifice for the future, they call it."

"A *damn* big sacrifice for the future," Father said. "I can't afford to gamble on just a chance."

"I know it," Grant answered. He spoke quietly and with patience. "But you'll have to anyway. If you don't, they'll dump it for you. You should have come and said what you had to say last night. It's too late now."

"What if it does shove the prices up?" Mother put in. "We get more and somebody else pays more. Where's the sense in that?"

"There isn't any," Merle said. "But we have to think of ourselves now. Somebody has to pay."

"What'll I do with a hundred gallons?" Father wanted to know. "Can we eat milk? read milk? wear milk? Not even the hogs can take that much!"

There was no way out of it, though, and we had to hold it all back. Even if we had tried not to join the rest, it would have been of no use. They lined up the roads and ditched over a hundred gallons. "One shout isn't enough," Grant said. "We've all got to roar together. The whole thing's no good if anyone backs out now."

"Give it away then," Mother said. "Give it out on the street. They oughtn't to stop you doing that!"

It was awful to see the milk lying around in tubs and barrels, overflowing the hog-troughs and souring in an afternoon. It made me sick almost to see Father driving the cows up every night, going through the hours of milking only to throw it out to the hogs. Grant couldn't stand it either, and the second day he piled the cans on a truck and said he was going to give it away. "Take it any old place," Father told him, half out of his mind with the waste and worry.

Grant left, and when he came back the cans were empty, and some had deep dents along the side. Father helped him to lift them out, and shook his head in a dazed way over the battered marks. "What happened?" he asked. "Who done this to my cans?" He ran his fingers over their sides as though they were alive.

"I gave it away in town," Grant told him.—"All but

the nine gallons Rathman ditched before I could pound in his head what it was I wanted to do. 'You'll bust up the strike!' he kept shouting, and made so much noise he couldn't hear anything that I said."

"Max has a head like a cannon-ball," Merle said. "What did you do to get words inside it?"

"Shoved him into the truck and took him along," Grant said. He laughed, but looked tired and worried.

"How's all this going to end?" Father wanted to know. "What hope've we got to win?"

"I don't know," Grant answered. "Hedden's in at the dairy now. Going to tell them that we can hold out forever. He's mud-poor himself, and if he don't sell he don't eat. We'll have to loan till it's over."

"Who's *we?*" Father shouted. "What've we got to give?"

Grant knew there was no use arguing, and knew that Father would give with the rest when the time came, so he started to move away. "If we lose," he said, "we'll have made a noise anyway. It'll be a good help later on to somebody else."

"Always the future!" Father went muttering to himself. "Always some other time! Always somebody else!—Ain't there no *now* for *us?*"

Grant piled up the cans and shut the gate. "First ploughing's hardest," he said. "Busts up the share sometimes. Maybe we'll get an ear of the crop, and maybe we won't." He knew there wasn't much hope.

4

WHETHER the strike was won or lost nobody ever was sure. Prices went up a cent and we started selling again, but there was another tax to pay and a change in the graded value which canceled the feeble rise. The quiet and masked way it was done drove Grant into a rage of helpless fury, but Father couldn't quite realize what had happened until he balanced his books at the month's end, and there was this three-day strike leaving an empty hole on the page. Even then he stayed up till twelve, going over and over the figures until the oil got so low the wick wouldn't burn, and he couldn't see anyway for being so tired.

It was from this time on that he seemed to trust Grant less; and things began going wrong between them.

The days went much alike, with a greenness still

left along the low places and the ironweed still strong. The sun came through a grey haze in the mornings, and then rose up red and triumphant to boil the earth again. I came to see its enormous and glaring eye with a stupid and helpless hate, and dreaded the mornings, but there were small intervals of peace and sometimes a few hours of coolness. On Sundays Father would leave his work—that is, did not plough or hay unless he had to. He did only the milking and cleaned his dairy rooms, which took all the morning, and then he had to get up the cows again at four. "Quite a day of rest!" Merle said. She did as much work herself, but managed to save out the afternoon, and we used to go back up through the pastures to where the old Borden church was, with its graveyard used for sheep-grazing now. They didn't have services there any more. Couldn't even afford one Sunday in the month. Nobody came except when they had to have funerals and dig a new grave. I used to go up and sit on the steps outside while Merle played on the ancient organ, the way Kerrin had done when we were little. I wondered sometimes if I should ever find answer to all the things I had asked myself that one time when we had gone ten years ago. . . .

The minister used to come once a month to preach, and for a whole year after we'd moved on the land Mother had wanted to go and hear him, but there always seemed something else that had to be done—always a calf or a meal or a jarring that could not wait —the farm like a querulous, sick old man whining for attention every hour. But we finally went one Sunday in June, a year and three months from the time we had come. Mother's church dress was faded and grown too big, but we thought it beautiful and important on account of the sleeves with some wilted pleats in front. Father refused to come, and sat on the porch staring after us with the Sunday paper in his hand. He looked saggy and tired, and acted as though he thought us a little coarse in going to church by ourselves without a man. "You children be good" was all he said, and stared off over our heads at a hawk. But Mother's face had a shined, expectant look, as though she were already kneeling in the church.

The roads were hub-high with sweet clover and wild roses spraying out in the dust. It was a warm day, and when we walked down the road it seemed as if larks flew up from every post, singing and yellow-vested. The fields were daisy-flooded and white with yarrow. A day almost too rich, too swamped with honeysuckle. When we came the church was already crowded, its yard full and trampled with wagons and old buggies. We went inside without stopping to talk to anyone, but Kerrin said that the church smelt musty, and hung around outside the door, hoping some fellow would speak to her, I guess. But they were all stuck together, like a gangling bunch of herons, out where the horses were. The women stared at her standing there alone, and after a while she came inside and sat down behind as though she belonged to some other family and not to us.

Merle looked at the organ with its shabby and familiar face, and whispered that it seemed different, more church-bound and primly humble than the times when Kerrin played it. She had used to sneak up in late afternoons or early mornings, and creep in through the unlocked window. Merle and I'd come with her sometimes and sit on the tombstones or the step while she played us wild hymns or queer uncertain jazz, forcing the poor old pipes to quaver with ungodly and pagan sounds. We wandered around deciphering the stones, and once found a locust clung to the Boggs' eroded stone, pulling his soft and pursy body over the names, hunting for foothold to free himself and split the thin scum of his shell. There were orange lilies growing wild around the graves, and black-eyed susans, but every Sunday before the minister came they were all slashed down and the graves trimmed back to a decent homeliness. When the organ got tired and its breath too asthmatic, Kerrin would come out and go home, striding on ahead of us like a red-haloed saint in the sun. We did not have to come and go with her at the time she chose, but always did, feeling a sort of undefined respect for anything that was older—in the way of years at least. We had come often to hear her play wild and invented pieces of her own that sounded like witches shrieking at each other, but this was the first time we had come to church and gone in at the front door with other people.

I stared across at the men and wondered if they would notice that I was there, but knew I was plain-sewn looking and the kind that an eye would look at without seeing, and I kept feeling the back of my head for fear that the braid-ends had come loose. I wondered why the people were here and if God was here, and the doubt and questioning began again—that doubt which had run like a tunneled stream, coming to surface at unforeseen and unwanted times before, and has gone through all the years afterward. . . . What had they come for, and did they believe what they heard, and did they live by it afterward at all? It was not the minister, a stupid and earnest little man, so much as the people coming to hear him that tormented and puzzled me. "Sin," shouted the little man, "is the cause of all the evil in the world. Sin is a wicked thing. Pray to be delivered from sin!" And for an hour he said the same thing over in other words and ways, but gave no explanation of what this evil thing might be. So at last when I came to see he was never going to tell us—either because he did not know or thought it would take too long—I began to look around and think of the people there, and if in what I knew and had heard of their lives there was any plan or pattern that could answer their being here.

I looked at the back of old Vigney Hickam with the green dress tight on her shoulder-blades, and her hair strained taut up to her hat. I wondered if what the minister said could mean anything to her, a spinster and living with old Mrs. Hickam a mile off the main road, and no chance to do any evil even if she had wanted to.—Unless it were cutting down fence-rows and ploughing up phlox, which I doubted the minister would have thought sins worthy of mention, being less colorful than adultery or fornication.

Joe Rathman and his wife were there, the old man lost like an ancient gnome in his great black suit, and not looking as though he were hearing a word of what was said.—Was probably sitting there patient and resigned, because he had sat there patient and resigned once a month all his life, and took this hour to reckon his chicken-savings. The three Rathman sons never came—big chuckmeat-looking boys of whom Father had said even then that Aaron was the best, and it was always of Aaron Mrs. Rathman talked. Their not being here gave me more to wonder and think about than if they had come and sat in an ox-like row. Aaron was different from the rest, with more shape to his face and less thickness between him and his feelings. He saw that things weren't always just black or white, but that there were shades between.

I looked at Miss Amy Meister whose brother had come back from the war and killed their father in one of his raging times, but she went on about her life just the same, raising bees and selling great yellow combs each fall, and knew more of evil and death than the minister ever had dreamed of in all his eighty years. But she sat there listening like a child while he talked of this formless sin. There was Stella Darden who'd married a tenant farmer and lived with his fourteen relatives in a one-room shack that wasn't much bigger than two outhouses—and hadn't any heat in winter, Aaron said, but what came out of themselves to warm the place. There was Leon Kind whose son had left him and gone away, not being able to stand the silence that Leon kept since his wife died. . . . And then I watched Mother sitting there, listening quiet, but more as though she were having some inner communion of her own, feeding and watering some faith of which the organ and church and minister were only the symbol and surroundings. She listened only to hear the sound of faith in his voice, and not to the words that meant little or nothing. I wanted to believe as she did, quietly, very steadfast, without reasoning or beyond reason, with a faith that seemed as much part of her as her hands or face. . . . But I never could. It was as though faith were a thing one was born with, like color or eyes or arms, and wouldn't be otherwise obtained.

When it came time for communion, Merle and I looked forward to having the little cups and crumbs, and wondered if it would be elderberry or wild-grape wine; and Mother's face had a rapt and luminous light about it, a sort of mystic anticipation as though she were worlds away. But before the taking began, we saw the deacon creep down the aisle toward Mother, and everyone's head turn around at once, pulled slyly and slow as by one big string. He leaned over and whispered behind his hand. "You'll have to get out," he said. "You don't belong to the church. Only church-members take communion." Mother stared at him, not understanding, and fumbled at her purse. "You'll have to get out," he said more loudly, and Kerrin punched Mother on the arm. "Let'm keep their old kraut-juice then!" she muttered, and started down the aisle. Mother said, "Oh, I see," and got up fast, nodding her head in a nervous way she had, trying to make him feel he had given no offence. People stared at us, curious and blank, and Vigney's mound of white daisies trembled on her head. We all got up and filed out behind each other, and Kerrin tried to bang the door shut, but it only swung back softly. You couldn't hear anything but the organ panting out *"It was there, it was there that I first saw the light, and the burden of my sins rolled away."*

We stood there outside and looked at each other, with the blank white face of the door behind us. I began to snicker, and Mother smiled but looked as if she had lost some irreplaceable thing and had been jerked back suddenly into life, and empty-handed. Then Kerrin, before we could stop her, yanked up a grass clump and smeared a cross-shaped stain on the door. "That for the pack of them!" she said. "Wormed old hickory-shells!" Mother was half out of her mind with horror, and tried to wipe it off with her under-skirt but only managed to blotch out the shape and leave a smudge of grey. There wasn't any water near, and Merle tried spitting on it but didn't help much, and then the organ stopped wheezing, and we were afraid someone would come out and find us all there, spitting and scrubbing on the door, so we walked off fast toward the road, Mother distracted and hot with sun, and Kerrin striding on tall ahead, pretending she did not know or belong to us.

"What did we do?" Merle kept asking. "Why're we different than other people?" But dust came up in hot clouds around us, and the sun was a drying fire, and nobody wanted to answer her. Nor would we have known what the answer was.

More now than ever, sitting there listening to Merle play and remembering that other Sunday, I wanted to know the reasons. And, more than that, wanted something outside myself. But a faith that would *fit* life, not just hide it. There was a great deal that I would have liked to believe. I would have liked to believe that whatever came to us was just, and be able to say like Wally Hutton's wife, rolling her eyes up piously, "The Lord gives and the Lord takes away," as she buried her seventh child like a bone for the feast of the Resurrection. It would be easier to bear the inevitable and just, if there were no way out. But surely, I thought, we have the right to live as fully as anyone else! Are we and all those around us—the Ramseys and Huttons and Meisters and all the rest—any worse than people who have no fear, no slough to fill, are not pawns to drouth and frost? Why were we chosen to be so stinted? . . . Perhaps if we could have been cut off from all seeing and hearing of those rare safe ones who had no need, we could have begun to blame it on God and be at peace. Knowledge is a two-edged knife, all blade, with no handle for even the owner to strike out with.

But it all came back to the same thing in the end, and I knew that no law or plan or freedom from debt could give me the one thing that I wanted more than all of the rest, and no law could make Grant love me.

5

BY JULY half of the corn was dead and flapped in the fields like brittle paper. The pastures burned to a cinder. I stumbled once in the woods and the ash of dry leaves flew up like a dust. Milk shriveled up in the cows. Prices went up, we heard again, but Dad got no more for his milk and got less for the cows he sold, since nearly all other farmers were selling off. The creeks were dry rock-beds then, hot stones that sent up a quiver in the air. The ponds were holes cracked open and glazed with a drying mud. I kept hearing the calves bawl all the time, hot and thirsty in the pastures, but could only water them in the evenings. We had to haul from a pond three miles away, and the horses got sores, even with rest when we borrowed Ramsey's mules. The heat was like a hand on the face all day and night. When everything was finally dead, I thought that relief from hope would come, but hope's an obsession that never dies.—Perhaps the ponds will fill up again . . . the fall pastures might come back with rain . . . the cistern get deep again. . . . There was still the awful torture of hope that would die only with life.

Merle alone didn't seem to mind the heat. She worked out in the fields with Grant and Dad, and was burned deep to a kind of smouldering brown. I noticed she grew more quiet in those days, not from the thing that was wasting Kerrin, draining her like black tallow: but something had started to worry her out of mildness. A sort of fear and responsibility. She tried to avoid Grant, and talked to him with a queer mixture of hesitancy and frankness. I pitied Grant and wondered if he was learning, as I had, the numbness of patience made possible only by blindly shoving away all doubt. He never complained, and sometimes I wished that he would say more. Shout or curse. His silence seemed like a wall against some rising flood.

Because I was quiet and dull I noticed Grant more than the others did, and sometimes even in the middle of talking he would seem years away from us and gone into himself. He was always kind; joked with us and praised the food, and asked sometimes for a special thing—for rice-balls or fritters with gravy. But even living day after day with him as we did and having to share the most trivial things, he seemed remote and grave, and there was a dignity about him that I loved.

It came on me suddenly once, with no reason for knowing, but with a certainty nothing could shake or change, that neither Mother nor Grant looked up to or envied any man. It was not a self-pride or a feeling of being different.—Not that at all. But a sort of faith in the dignity of the human spirit. I only stumble for words to make this plain. It is not a thing to be trapped in little letters and spelled for children. I only know it was there and gave them an inch of height beyond us; and that they were never petty or even ridiculous, though often mistaken enough, I guess.

After a while we had less work, so much of the garden stuff having died, and the ground was too hard for ploughing. We sat out and talked on the nights too hot for sleep and too dark for reading or work. There wasn't much new to read even if there had been light to see. Merle never complained about this and, re-reading all of the old books, pretended to get more out of the fourth time than the third. Only once I heard her break out in exasperation, throwing away some grease-marked history of early battles. "God's name!" she said. "Why can't we get something written after the prophets died!—Something that doesn't taste of Adam. I want to know what people are saying *now!*"

"The same things they always did, I guess," Mother said. "Only maybe they've got a new *way* of saying it now."

"A new way might help some," Merle had answered. She'd looked more tired than I'd ever seen her, and did not pick up the book or smile. "It doesn't fit to be scraped like this, with God or Something squeezing us into boxes marked 'Extra small'! We can't grow in the dark like fungus does.—If I thought this would always be, I—" She didn't finish, but sat there drumming her fingers up and down in a helpless way. After all, she'd known there was little use in shouting.

These nights when we sat and talked in the dark she tried to dredge Grant of everything that he knew, or had heard or read or seen. "What did they look like there?" she'd ask him. "What did they say? What did they read? . . . If the man had won, why didn't they give him the prize? Because his name didn't signify! His name!—That's strange.—That's hard to understand. . . . Well, what did he say? How did he look? How does a person take injustice like that?—'Takes it hard and quiet. Takes it like a rock,' you say! That's no way to do; that's no way at all! A man ought to shout, ought not to suffer and be dumb! . . . Well, what did they wear when the time had come?—No color? no robes?—Black! Only black? What person would dress in black when they had the money for red? Good Lord, one might as well have no money at all! Might as well be a dairy farmer! . . . What did they have to eat and how did they serve it? Was it meat they had? or fish, or what?—You don't remember? You've forgotten already what they had? You're worse than a book half-blotted out. A person ought to remember all that he sees. Ought to be an enormous sponge of things! . . ."

"Leave him alone," Father would say at last. "Ain't you ever satisfied, Merle?"

But Merle had her answer always ready. "Not till I'm deaf and dumb and blind," she would say triumphantly. "Not till I'm ploughed down under corn!"

Grant always liked to answer her questions, though and would sit there quietly, leaning his back against the rickety pillars and trying to relive again in words all the other years of his life. I think if he could he would have remembered the color of sky on such and such a day, and the name of the station clerk in each town that he'd wandered through. He tried to rake up every legend or tale that he'd ever read to please her, and sometimes I'd come on him standing alone, a half-opened gate forgotten under his hand, searching his mind for the names and place of some memory brought back by a sudden sound or smell, or recalled by some unimportant word.

Kerrin would come these evenings and lie half-asleep in the porch's shadow; some nights not saying a word, and other times very shrilly excited. She would interrupt Grant and tell us things she'd picked up around on the farms.—Scandals half true and half invented, of how old Leon Kind, who'd been going strange, had watered his dying garden with milk—poured out nine gallons still warm from the buckets over his shriveled beans. She told us of how she had seen a light moving along Miss Vigney's lane at twelve; and Miss Vigney, who never stayed up after dark for fear of using her oil and candles, had left something burning in her window, and one could see her shadow against the blind. These things were true, she would swear: she had heard from someone who knew, she had seen them herself. She had a way of retelling that made them seem strange and sinister and a little vile. When she heard of a death or accident, she was never at peace until she knew every circumstance of how it had come to be. And somehow out of her words one got a picture of restlessness and fear widening and spreading through all the farms. Out of poverty fear, and fear bringing hate; and out of hate a sly violence, and sometimes insanity or death. She slurred the patience we knew was there, and never spoke of a saner planning that might in time change all our shrunken lives.

I was glad of the evenings, even of those when Kerrin talked in her fast and half-ghoulish way. They kept me from sleep, and in sleep I dreamed too much. The dreams were always alike, never as strange or beautiful as Merle's, nor as terrible as hers, but monotonous and true. They were nothing more than a living again of the days, with the quiet desires and fears spoken aloud and received as they might have been in life. Never in all the dreams was the moment of happiness complete, or even the point of madness or pain quite reached. They ended always just on the margin of some great evil or ecstasy, and I would wake up hot and cold, and stiff as one dead, and see Father groping along the hall in the early light.

But there was one dream I remember which was different from most and stayed alive in my mind for days. I was standing alone at the foot of the pasture hills, and could see Grant coming toward me across the barren creek-bed, and the grass was scorched all around us to its edge. I could see him walking plainly and knew it was Grant, but his face was blurred and though I kept straining my eyes and stared up when he reached me, I never could see his face. "Is that you, Marget?" he asked. "Has Merle gone?" He spoke as if blind and not seeing me either. "She's here," I said. "She's always here. She always will be, I guess." "I don't see her," Grant said. "There's only rock here, and sheep marks in the dust." I looked around and could see her nowhere myself, but I told him she was here where the rock was, or gone for only a little while.

Then Grant started to go and said there was no use in his waiting. "You stay," he said. "Take it all. Accept and take everything. Take it hard to you." I put out my hand to stop him. "Take what?" I asked. Then he turned and came back and I could see that his hands were open and that he was looking straight at me. And for a moment I saw his face plainly as though noon sun were on it. And then I woke up; and the house was as quiet as a tomb, dark-still, and only a dog barking miles away.

It had been so real that all the day after I'd wanted to stop Grant and ask him what the thing was he had never finished, and for a while part of the dream's own strangeness seemed clung around him. I felt some way that now I knew him better than anyone else ever had, and it was a pleasant thing to pretend for a while.

6

THE drouth went on. Trees withered, the grass turned hay, even the weeds dried into ashes, even the great trees with their roots fifty years under ground. Burdock and cockle were green near the empty creek-bed, but the giant elms began to die. The limas died, lice on their blossoms, convolvulus strangling the string-bean bushes, and the carrots so bound in earth that nothing could budge them from the ground.

I walked some nights in the hay fields hoping to find a cooler air, and the desire for rain came to be almost a physical hurt. I could not feel any more the immensity of night and space, that littleness we speak of feeling before the stretching of fields and stars. I felt always too big and clumsy and achingly present. I could not shrink.

And then one noon when it seemed that we could not stand it any longer, that we should dry and crack open like the earth, there was a sudden blast of cold air and in the north we saw an enormous bank of rising clouds. The air had been hot and still, storm-quiet and dark; but for a week clouds ominous and storm-surfed had been covering the sky and dissolving into nothing. The sunsets were clear and crystal as after a great rain, but not one drop had fallen. Now we saw the clouds tower up and reach forward like great waves, and there was the bull-mumbling of thunder. It had come up fast and still, no warning except the quiet, and we stood there staring like blocks of stone. Then Merle shouted, "It's here!" and ran out fast like a crazy person, and we saw stabs of lightning all through the black upboiling mass. Dad looked at Mother, and I saw the awful unmasking of his face, as if all the underground terror and despair were brought to the surface by his hope, and I felt a jab of pity and love for him stronger than I'd ever known before. Mother snatched up a bucket and put it out on the stones, half-wild to think that a drop might escape or go where it wasn't needed. We dragged out buckets and saucepans, even grabbed up bowls and put them out on the window-sill, and Merle pulled Grant's drinking-cup down from the nail. It got darker and a fierce wind whipped our clothes, and Merle was wild with excitement and the cold rushing of air. We saw Kerrin running up from the barn, lashed back and forth like a willow switch, and the sheep poured down along the road in a lumpy flood, baaing and crying toward the barn. I wanted to run and shriek, get wings and flap like the swooping crows. Grant looked ten years younger, shouted and called like a boy. We all looked at each other and felt burst free, poured out like rain. "Bring up the tubs," Father shouted. "She's coming, all right! She's here, I tell you!" He ran toward the cellar steps just as the first drops fell, hard-splashing and wide apart. He staggered back up with the wash-tubs, and the drops struck down like a noise of hammers on hollow tin. There was a wonderful brightness on Mother's face, a sort of light shining from it, almost a rapt and mystic look as she stood there with flower-pots dangling from her hand.

Those first drops scattered a few dead leaves on the vine and sank out of sight in earth. In the north a rift of blue widened and spread with terrible swiftness. The storm clouds loomed high and went on south. No more drops fell, and a long pole of sunlight came down through the clouds. A burnt and ragged hole in the clouds with the sun's eye coming through. We could feel the wind dying already, leaving only a cooler air. No rain.

Father's knees seemed to crumple up under him and he sat down heavy on the steps.

"God's will be done!" Kerrin said, and burst out laughing. "What're the barrels for, Grant?"

"Tubs to catch sunlight in," he answered her, "—storing up sweet light for the dark!" He looked fierce and haggard, sweat dry on his face from the wind, and a wire-cut ragged across his cheek like a lightning mark. Kerrin started to laugh again and threw up her arms. She looked queer and ridiculous, and I saw how thin she'd gotten, her neck like a twist of wire, and the wind seemed to blow through her bones. It made my heart sick to look at her. Grant turned away and shaded his eyes toward the sun. "Damned old Cyclopean eye!" he muttered. Stared up hating and helpless at the sky.

The clouds moved out and apart. Enormous stretches of sky were clean as glass. The thunder sounded a long way off, almost unheard. . . . Nothing was changed at all.

7

CHRISTIAN RAMSEY came up that night. Father was lying out on the porch half-asleep, and had not spoken a word since the storm passed over. Kerrin said almost nothing either, only watched Grant. The coolness was gone and the wind smothered already. I think it is strange how much the mind can endure and still hold on to its shell of sanity. Does too-great fear annul itself? Too much sickness cancel pain? . . .

An awful patience seemed to come over us, a numbness that was in itself a kind of death.

Christian looked like a ragged skeleton in the moonlight, his eyes and cheek-bones dim white marks. Merle woke up Father who stared at Ramsey, not knowing the man at first. I pushed a chair toward him, but Ramsey kept on standing there, one hand picking at the porch rail. Father sat up and peered at him through the dark. "What didja come for, Ramsey?" he asked, his voice suspicious and hard, but with an exhausted falling at the end.

"We got to git off the farm," Ramsey said. He swallowed his voice in a nervous mumble and it made Father angry because he had to strain hard to hear all the words. "I come up tonight because the crop's gone for sure. Lucia says it is done for sure. We thought it would rain certain this time. We waited all day and nothing come." He pulled something small and crumpled out of his pocket and held it up. "This a potato-stalk. Look like an ol' dry weed!"

"So's everyone's," Father said. "Corn's gone. Everything's blasted. I can't help you."

"It's the rent," Christian said. "We ain't a farm if

we can't pay up. It's a year behind now. I thought maybe you-all—"

"You thought wrong, I reckon, Ramsey." Father turned himself over with his back to Christian. "I'd help you some if I had it, but I ain't. I can pay my own, but I ain't a cent to spare."

"—A loan, I mean," Ramsey said. "We'd pay it back next year maybe." He couldn't seem to believe that Father had understood and was still refusing him.

"If I had it I'd loan it, Ramsey," Dad said, short and tired. "I haven't got it. That's all."

"But what'll I do?" Christian burst out desperate. "We ain't no place to go! Lucia don' want to live no place else. We want to stay here and live!"

"Got any relatives?" Father asked. "Won't anyone else loan you money round here?"

Ramsey stared at the ground and shook his head. "I been every place before. I been up to the county, but they tol' me so long as I don' need food that I got to manage."

Dad sat up and wiped his face. "I'm sorry, Ramsey," he said. "There ain't anything I can do." He got up and lurched inside the door, bent over like a mound.

Ramsey stared after him. I was glad it was dark and we could not see his face and the horrible stricken look that must be there. Then he turned and started to shuffle off, talking confusedly to himself in a black bewildered mutter.

There was nothing that any of us could do or say. Nothing at all. Dad was right. We had no money to spare. Food,—but food wouldn't pay off rent. We had not bought anything for two months then, not even sugar except for canning. . . . I could hear Merle crying when he'd gone, and even Kerrin looked sick.

8

GRANT went up to Turner's next morning, but might as well have saved his time. "Ramseys don't make good tenants," Turner said. "Don't know how to get most off the farm. Anyone else'd have managed." Grant told him nobody'd managed this year, but he only smiled. "He wasn't cruel," Grant said. "Not cruel like a boy gouging toad eyes out. It's only that he hasn't a mind,—his imagination a hollow. He 'saw,' he 'quite understood,'—but he didn't really see anything at all. I said, 'You don't understand what it means to Ramsey!'—God! I didn't know how to put it in words and make the old man see! 'Ramsey's worked all his life on the land,' I said. 'Nine children now . . . no relatives . . . no place to go. . . .' But Turner just sat there like an egg, a stone! 'Niggers make poor tenants,' he'd keep saying. 'A white man would have managed.' Then I got mad and asked if he thought being niggers kept rain off their land, but he only grinned. Said he needed the rent and was 'making plans.' Ramsey is not included in these 'plans.' "

"They'll have to get out then?" Mother asked. "There's nothing more to be done?"

"Only the moving," Grant answered. More bitter than I'd ever seen him before.

"You should have hit him a good one, Grant!" Merle said. "Given him one for me. Hit him so hard he'd never have bounced back up again."

"He wouldn't have bounced," Grant muttered sourly. "He'd have crumpled up into dust. Dry rot."

To us the horror of this poverty lay in the fear and the scraping that left mind and soul raw and quick to infection; but to Mother it was the shame of being unable to help, of standing by bound and helpless and seeing life make its assault on others. . . . And there was nothing to do this time but watch.

9

THE last evening of July we sat out on the porch, quiet, Father thumbing over the almanac in search of August rains. Grant came up while we were there, dumped down his pails and went over to look at the barometer the way Merle does every evening, as if there was still some power in the broken old thing to bring down rain instead of marking always the "Clear and Dry."—She used to shake it sometimes, but the weather-hand never moved. Grant saw me watching, and grinned, knowing I'd seen him peer at it only an hour ago when he came up for the buckets. "It might of changed—you can't always tell," he said. He was burned out, heat-hollowed but still big, his craggy cheek-bones broadened out and jutting where flesh was drained away. "You get to work," he said. "Don't spy on a person's failings! There's a kind of haze, anyway, I noticed—" I knew it was only dust and so did he, but my mind was too shrunk to think of an answer, and he'd given up waiting for me to talk back the way Merle did, and pretended he wanted none.

He sat down by me and we stared off into the valley-greyness. A sort of dull purple began to wash up its walls, and the one creek pool was a tarnished brass. But along the bluffs there was still a late red light on the stones. We sat there together but earths apart, his thoughts as always on Merle, and I knew I had only to wait and he'd say something of her soon. And I sat there wondering if ever while still alive I'd be rid of this old and familiar pain. ancient as life—love without return or hope, but unaltered by any change. . . . He sat stooped over as though he had found how much harder resistance makes those things which are inevitable anyway, and there was about him the almost shameful tiredness that comes of heat and not labor. Then I saw I was wrong when he turned to get up, and that all of the still defiance and tautness was there inside. Rod-stiff and quiet. Refusing stubbornly to accept life on its own terms and make for himself a dreary peace. He'd take what came for a while—but not always.

A small breeze came up and moved the dead leaves on a vine—it was almost cool in the dry stillness—

and then died. "It'll come back," Dad said. "It's more than the valley farmers have. Down in the bottom-land they've got no wind at all." He took off his hat and laid it on the steps, mopped at his wet hair growing thin and the red scalp shining damp through. He seemed more cheerful in a way, like a man who had touched bottom, going down through so much that no more seemed possible, and had begun to hope.

There was no sound. Only once the dry bawling of a thirsty steer a long way off toward Rathmans'. The breeze came up again, moving Grant's wet hair. "Nights ain't so hot as they were," Dad spoke again. "Almost cold down by the stream."

"Next year'll be different," Mother said. "I've never known drouth for three years straight together. Corn ought to bring more with the shortage."

"It *might,*" Dad said. He had come after these ten years to say nothing positively or to predict. We always said "ought" or "might," and seldom "will." There was a hope though, even if feeble and a long way off, and it made the heat and the death that was all around us seem less, and a slow, reluctant cooling came in the air. The fog of purple crawled up high on the bluffs, blotted the stream-bed and the firs. Next year . . . another lease of hope . . . a chance even to lay something by with a margin over. This drouth had happened. It was here and it could not happen again. Earth would compensate somehow for this dry hell and withering. . . .

Suddenly Grant got up and walked out a way in the yard. He stared off south down the road, and we saw two mules with a wagon, blurred by their own dust and crawling painfully slow.

"Ramsey's mules," Grant said.

Dad peered through his dusty glasses and asked where Ramsey'd be going at this hour. "Must be wrong, Grant," he said. "Ramsey's no time to ride around—no business to on a week-day."

"Ramsey's got all the time he wants now," Grant said. "More than he'll ever use." But Dad didn't understand.

The wagon came nearer and we saw that Christian was driving, bent over and holding the reins as if half-asleep. Lucia sat up beside him, enormous and overflowing the seat, Mac in her arms asleep and dirty. The other children were back in the wagon, crammed between boxes and things that might have been kindling or chairs. They stared at us gravely, Henry's face puffed and drawn out with crying. One of the little girls waved. They stopped at the gate, sweat running down off the mules' hide, and the hair wet-black on their faces under the socket hollows. One had a harness-sore big as a hand across his rump, black on the edge but red where the flies were.

"Turner kicked him out," Grant said. "He couldn't scratch up the rent."

Dad looked at him and said, "I see," as one who neither believed nor understood, but wanted us to think that he did. It came as a sort of shock, though Ramsey meant nothing to him.

Grant went out with me to the gate. The children were queer and solemn, and even Lucia looked old. "Gawd-damned ol' alligatah nosed us out, Mistah Koven. Sent his man ovah and said not to make no trouble. Nevah come hisse'f or I'd a smash a stove off top his head. He knowed it, too!" Henry climbed down over the wheel and put his hand in Grant's. He looked up solemnly and picked his nose. Grant asked if they had any place to go, but Ramsey shook his head. "Stay in Union somewhere. Lucia might git wuk in the fact'ry there." He stared down at the mules and did not turn his head to look at us; sullen and hopeless, making anything that we said seem hollow. "We got ol' Mooh still," Henry whispered, and pointed to Moore's ghost-body tied to the wheel by a dirty string. *"He* wanta kill'm, but Mom say no, you keep'm foh chillen!"

Ramsey lifted the reins and straightened up, flicked at the mules and spoke to Henry.—Not angrily, but as though nothing mattered much and he had only remembered to call him from long habit. Grant picked Henry up and wedged him next to the rusty bed. The wagon was filled with stuff that looked like a junk-man's leavings. Paula sat on a pile of rusty cans and held in her arms an old tire-tube, blasted and full of holes. "Shoe-patchin's," Henry told us. Under the sacks and furniture the back was piled with corn.

"We took'm," Lucia said. "Chrishun owe everything to Mistah Turner, so we stole all we could fit in a wagon and took'm along. He gonna come fetch the mules when we git hauled, but said he don' want the wagon. That's all the corn that came to ear."

"Going to sell it?" Grant asked her. "You won't have anything left to feed it to."

Lucia grinned. "Going to keep her, Mistah Koven. Corn keeps a long time. Might git us some chickens an' a hawg some day. Then we'll have somethin' to feed'm with!" She sat up confident and serene-looking. "Tell your folks goodbye, Miss Marget. Goodbye, yohse'f. Goodbye, Mistah Koven!"

Christian jerked at the reins, and they started crawling forward again. Henry waved wildly, standing up in the wagon and leaning over the edge. The children shrieked goodbye and Lucia waved her hand.—Enormous and black and her face twisted up in a sudden flood of crying.

The mules crept around the turn where the blasted cornfield was, and were out of sight.

"That's what will happen to us," I was thinking. "We'll go back crawling the same way we came."

"Poor old Lucia!" Grant said. "I wish that she'd had her crack at Turner!"

10

THAT same week Old Rathman fell and broke his hip. Grant went over next day and stayed awhile to help them.—Max had married his Lena, and brought her home to live on account of the rent being free, but was away all day himself, and the rest of the boys were gone now. Old Rathman had gone up to bed, Grant told us, and one of his dizzy spells came on and he fell. The old lady heard him and went up and tried to haul him on the bed but couldn't lift him, and then went down where Max had just come in and was starting to eat his supper. "Max," she'd said, "when you finish supper, come help me lift Pop up on the bed." They didn't know till the doctor came that he'd broken his hip in two places.

"The old man puttered around too long—had head-spinnings before," Father said. "Won't never quit work till he can't lift a hand or foot."

—*Like you,* I wanted to say. Father wasn't well and he worked too hard. I wished he had some of Mother's sanity and would take things slower. It's wrong to waste life for the living's sake. She felt things as much as he did, wanted comfort, and yet could more easily do without. A curious warm aliveness under and over some inner core that was not attached to it . . . more wholly alive because less dependent on life. . . .

Grant told Dad he was going to help at Rathman's a couple of mornings. Three acres of melons the old man had left. Blood-ripe and had to be hauled in a day, otherwise there'd be nothing but fields of pulp.

"I don't pay you to help at Rathman's," Father said, forgetting he never paid Grant anyway. They sat out muttering on the steps while we worked inside. Grant's big shadow cast out longer than Father's down the path from the kitchen light. We could hear what they said, but they talked as if we didn't exist. Although I doubt that even in these times Grant was entirely unaware of Merle's walking back and forth in the room behind him, shoving her kettles on and off the stove.

"I don't ask you to pay me," Grant said.

"And Max won't neither," Dad answered. "Max don't pay anybody but himself."

"He can't quit his job," Grant said. "Somebody's got to be the goat. We can't cut here tomorrow, anyway. There's nothing ready."

"There ain't nothing *ever* going to be ready, either," Dad said. "Ironweed-hay and a silo full of grasshoppers."

"We should have grown melons, too," Kerrin said. She spoke out of the dark where she'd stood there listening, and waited for Grant to say she was right, but he only answered something about hill country and no rain. Dad sat up and turned at her. "Nothing ever right, is it? Nothing ever done right like other people!" He got up and shuffled off to the barn. "You go ahead," he rumbled back at Grant. "You go do what you want."

Kerrin came and sat down where he'd been by Grant. She sat near him in a kind of hungry and yet hesitating way, but he didn't move or turn toward her, only stared off after Dad.—Poor crazy Kerrin! All that she did I wanted at times to do, but had more sense or less courage—I do not know which it was.

11

OLD RATHMAN'S accident had seemed a sudden and awful thing, wrenching away the thickness of their comfort and leaving them now no better off than the rest of us. Even worse off, perhaps.

I went over one day two weeks later and talked a long time with Mrs. Rathman back up in the orchard out of sight of the house. She looked very old, sagged and pouched and shrunk of all life. "That Lena!" she said. "I haven't speak to her for two weeks now! I talk to Max but not to her. I picked nine boxes of lima-beans and have them all ready and these people call up and ask for them and Lena says no, she ain't time to take them in, she's got her washing to do, and she's done enough for me and Pop, she says, and I ain't any way to get in town, with Max gone all day and Pop sick in bed, and the boxes had to set there and shrivel till they weren't even fit for the crows to eat. Then she comes, asks me for money to pay the 'lectric bill, the telephone bill—the taxes she wants to have me pay—and I asked her where the money was she and Max got off of Pop's berries that they took and stripped and sold before I got any of a few I was saving for the kind of wine that he likes, and Lena said she didn't know nothing about it, and Max said he lost on all them berries and got less than the cost of hauling, so he just kept the money and paid on the car with it—that same money he got from the berries.—And sometimes she says, 'We don't want to stay here no longer. It's too Gottdamn hot upstairs anyway,' and I tell her she should go then, but they won't because it's cheap here and I don't charge them no rent, and she asks me what I would do if she and Max went and Pop sick and all the boys gone, and I said I'd manage easy and could do all right without her, but she didn't have anything to say because they ain't anywhere else they can go for nothing, and their car ain't paid for, I know, because a man called up here one day before I had the telephone took out when they wouldn't pay, and I answered it and he wanted to know when they were going to make their month-payment, and I said, 'They ain't nothing to pay with, so you don't need to expect!' and shut off on him. And they got debts all over the county for this and that, and Max borrow ten dollars last night, but I might as well have give him it for a gift!"

She was lonely, too, she told me, and said that the other boys didn't come out on Sundays like they used to, because Lena didn't have anything to do with them and looked mad and sag-faced when they came, and went off upstairs and ate by herself; and Hilda didn't come out much either, because Lena acted so nasty to her once on account of Hilda's opening up the new ice-box door—the one that wasn't paid for—just to see what she kept there, and Lena went into a rage and quarreled with her like she did with Max till, Mrs. Rathman said, she couldn't stand it much longer.

She told me all this in a single pouring, as one who'd been shut inside too long, and all her mild comfortableness was gone. I think she was glad to have me listen, although there was little that anyone could do or say. The farm looked going-apart, too, sliding to seed—the pond choked with water-lilies and the berry rows overgrown—with Max gone so much and the boys coming only once in a while, and Old Rathman not able to do anything but eat and shout and get his bed dirty, not knowing half the time what he did.

I went back up the road, Old Rathman's voice crying and shouting in my ear, and wondered if there was peace or safety anywhere on the earth.

12

IN AUGUST the smell of grapes poured up like a warm flood through the windows. But they ripened unevenly, with hard green balls all through the purple. The apples fell too soon, crackling in the dry grass,—gold summer apples mushed and brown, and the sour red winesaps with white flesh. The creek stopped running altogether, and the woods were full of dead things—leaf-dust and thorny vines brittle to the touch. It was chill and quiet sometimes in early mornings, but the heat returned, the sun blasting and fierce as ever, and the red plums fell like rain in the cindered grass. In places the grasshoppers left nothing but the white bones of weeds, stripped even of pale skin, and the corn-stalks looked like yellow skeletons. Most of the garden was lost. Even potatoes were black as after a frost or fire. The cucumbers curled up and wrinkled. Tomatoes rotting, with pale and smelly skins. The beans bleached and colorless.

Day after day it went on. Hot wind, hot sun, hot nights and days, drying ponds and rivers, slowly, carefully killing whatever dared to thrust up a green leaf or shoot. Only the willows lived.

There were times when I wanted to crumple up like an ash, or scream. It was unbearable, I tell you! Death in the hot wind, in the blazing sunlight and dry air. The fields scorched white.

I saw the early goldenrod bloom feebly, like drifts of yellow pollen along the fence-rows, and I remembered that there was a time—it seemed a hundred years back—when the sight of goldenrod was enough to live and feed on. But now in these days it was only a blur beyond the thought of potatoes and the blasted fields and Kerrin's increasing vagueness.—She had gone back to teach when school started in August, but seemed still uncertain of what she wanted, furious and balked that she could not reach or do things of which she had no clear idea herself.

And then when it seemed that no worse or more terrible thing could come to us, there was another.

The Huttons called us one morning. Asked if we could get word sent over to Kerrin's school and have Whit Hutton come home. His uncle'd been killed, they said. The hay-hoist had broken and fallen on top of him. No ma'am, there was nothing that we could do. Just tell Whit to come right home.

It was a long walk up to the school, and I wondered sometimes, plodding those miles of dust and living each moment only for the times when a tree cast its thin dry shade, why there was always such hurry with everyone to spread the news of a death. Why should we have to know so soon? Why was I struggling here through the hot noon sun so that Whit could know, only a few hours sooner, something the knowing of which would help neither him nor anyone else? Always when someone dies, before even their eyes are closed the bitter knowledge of it is rushed to those who will care the most, as though they who witnessed the death grudged even a half-hour's kind oblivion to the rest. Besides, I knew Whit Hutton's uncle, and knew that if a hay-hoist had fallen and smashed his head to a bloody pod it was because he had been too drunk to know where his feet were standing, and that now there was at least one less for Stella to feed and shove out at night. But now there would be a big funeral, and Wallace, who skirted a church all his life and passed it by like a quicksand-bog, would be laid with the other Huttons under a hideous family monument, the shadow of which looked always like a monstrous slop-pail squatting above the graves.

There was no reason to hurry. Wally could not go off any more. Time now, hours of time for Whit to see the splunged-in head of his uncle and fill his ears with the story of how it happened, muttered and shrilled to him in a dozen ways. Back there in the time when Wally was still alive and making a gin-coated, sound-proof shield between himself and the hard necessity of thought—back there was the time for hurry. But only a man with a blue-gulched head and his slovenly heart stopped permanently at last could set anyone in motion. I wondered what it would mean to Whit—a holiday and a sort of eminence over the others, an extra slice of bread in the mornings now that fat old Wally had lost his appetite. Good mulch for a cornfield, Grant had said of him once. Things happened suddenly. Not when we fear or pray for them most, but not without cause or link somewhere if we could trace the invisible design. But was this so, after all? Suppose Grant should die? Where then would the pattern be? I could not think any longer of these things,—not when I really cared—not when the thought alone made my heart dry up like earth.

The woods were stripped of leaves and underbrush. Locust trees thin and thorny, gnawed white with grasshopper mouths, and the trumpet-vines were naked of leaves. The cornfields looked as they did in late November.

The schoolyard grass was dusty, worn bare as a chicken yard in patches, and the shadeless windows were grimy with finger marks. I walked up quiet and stood in the door. None of us had been over to Kerrin's school since it had opened this year. It was too hard to think up a way of coming that would not seem like spying. There would have been nothing more raw or suspicious-looking than for one of us to have come, reasonless, just to hear her teach. But she had been even worse this month and we were worried, wondering how she taught and what went on at the school. Early in August she had been more restless than ever and had gone sometimes with Grant when he took the milk to Union. But she never remembered the messages that we gave her, and delayed his coming back home again. Nor did she seem any happier in having gone away from the farm awhile; she said that nothing in Union differed much from what was out in the barns. She'd seemed glad at first to be back at school, but was queerly reluctant to tell about her teaching. She talked at first a good deal about entertainments the children were going to give, and would sit with her face dark and intent as if she were thinking out all the plays and recitals in her mind. "I've got to plan," she'd keep saying, and then stare off at the air, forgetting about it all. She refused to tell us how things went on, what the children said or did. "They learn. I see that they learn, all right. What else is to say? What is it you want to know?—how the room smelt?—who kicked who?—how dumb Hutton's kids can be? Maybe you'd like a diagram of their dirt!" Then she'd go off and leave us, refusing to talk any more. Mother'd begun to look strained and depressed, as if something were going back on her and peace getting harder and harder to find. She watched Kerrin, knowing how useless it was to try and talk with her or come near to even the rim of truth unless Kerrin unconsciously betrayed it. "You ought to go over and see her sometime at school," she told me. "Think of some reason for going there while she's at work."

But till now there had been no reason. And I wished to God sometimes afterward that there had never been any excuse for going. . . . Kerrin was at the desk, but didn't see me. She stared down at her book and mumbled out questions to the class. It was hot almost to oven-heat under the roof, and her hair was damp, lay flat on her head like a heavy scum. She asked the questions fast without looking up and not waiting to hear the answers given. "That's right," she'd say, and go on to the next one. The children squirmed or slept in their seats, but did not whisper. It was queer—their silence and Kerrin's not looking up. Even here in the shadowless light of full sun there was something about it all that made me cold and sick. It came to me that they were *afraid* to talk. They were used to her doing this!

For five minutes Kerrin rushed on with her questions, then slammed the book shut quickly. She looked up and saw me without at first knowing who it was. I saw the blood wash up her face in a tide and go away leaving only the soiled, burnt color of her skin. She was angry and nervous as if she'd been caught in some nasty thing. "When did you sneak up here? Who sent you?" she kept asking before I had a chance to say. She came to the door, and her thin face looked blotched and ugly out in the glaring light. Even when I explained to her why I'd come, and she called out Whit to tell him, it was more the shock of my coming than the news of Old Wally's death that concerned her. "Who sent you?" she asked. "What'd you sneak up here for? Why didn't they come themselves?"

When Whit came outside she told him to go on home. "Your folks called up. You've got to go home." The boy looked scared and sullen, and didn't seem to believe her. "Your uncle's dead," she told him. "Hay-hoist knocked him off." She seemed almost to take a malicious delight in telling it to him that way. Whit stared at us, then started off down the road like a crazy rabbit. I called out after him not to run, that he'd die in the sun, but he didn't hear.

"Wally won't leave!" Kerrin shouted. "He'll wait—

no need to hurry!" She burst out laughing, then turned back at me. "The show's over," she said. "You don't have to hang around any more, do you? Or maybe you'll think up something else to say?"

"That's all," I said. "I have to go back right now. I could have waited to let him know, but they'd have been angry—outraged—if he hadn't gotten the message now.—What's wrong with my coming, Kerrin?" I knew it was useless to ask her this—that she was beyond all questioning—but I couldn't resist, couldn't keep back this last attempt to treat her as one who could still hear reasoning. It only made her more angry, though.

"You wanted to see if I was here, wanted excuse to see me teaching! Whit could have waited. You just wanted to come and watch me.—That's all that you ever do anyway, just watch and spy over people.—You'd be afraid to do anything yourself! What've you ever done that's hard? What've you ever known but your everlasting baking and books?—your sweet little leaves and weeds!" Her voice kept getting louder till it was almost a shout. Loud and foolish out in the dusty yard. Then before I could answer she turned inside and shut the door.

I went back down the road, forgetting even the dust and heat. I remember now the elm-saplings' dusty grey and the naked vines, but could think of nothing but Kerrin then.

When I told Mother what I'd seen, she didn't say anything at first, but just sat down on the porch, too tired and heavy to stand any longer. It was six o'clock but the sun was still hot as noon, the vines dead on the pillars—only strings left with a few dry leaves. When the cows moved near the barn, dust flew up in thick clouds and settled back ankle-deep in the hoof marks.

"We ought to tell them now," Mother said at last. "If she isn't teaching their children. If she isn't responsible any more."

"They'll find it out soon enough," I said. "She'll never listen to us. There's nothing that we can do or say. They'll find it out from the children and make her go." It sounded crude and indifferent, put in words. It was the truth, but the truth without all the fear and meaning and worry that lay underneath it. We could feel so much, but talk only in bald plain words together. I had a quick and unbearable vision of how things were going to be when Kerrin was home all day, made worse by the humiliation of being asked to go. I wondered, too, how we were going to do without her money. Poor Dad, harassed with debt and drouth already, would have to find some substitute for her crabbed but welcome dole. There was enough hate, enough fear, without this coming, too—one thing following another until it seemed impossible to suffer more. I remembered the awful words in *Lear:* "The worst is not so long as we can say 'This is the worst.'" Already this year I'd cried, This is enough! uncounted times, and the end had never come.

"Tomorrow you'll have to go see the board," Mother said. "They'll have to find someone else for her place."

I wished that tomorrow would never come.

13

I WENT because there was nothing else to do. But all the way in the dust and heat I was dragged with the desire to turn back. Let her go on till she was found out some other way.—Let the children tell, or someone else find the way things were.—Take the money for this month and the next and the next,— take it until they found her out in another way. And I knew horribly in my own heart that I should never have told of my own accord or if the decision were left to me alone.

I told Mr. Bailey she wasn't well or able to teach the children any more, and that if he went to the school he'd understand. I wanted to say, "Let it come from you. Don't let her know that we told you!" But I knew that we'd have to take all blame in the end, and might as well have it from the beginning.

He wouldn't believe me at first, and even resented that I should question their choice, feeling perhaps that it cast a stain on himself and all the board. And then he got angry in a quick blind way, having all of men's instinctive dread and revolt against the strange, his mind jumping to violence and asylums and fear for the children. He treated me as if I too were tainted, and asked why we hadn't told before. "We didn't know," I said, and tried to explain the way things were. It was nothing to be afraid of, I said; they'd just have to get someone new for the place.

. . . I came back sick through, dreading how Kerrin would act, and thinking of all the days we'd have to spend with her, piled one on top of the other without relief or change. And the salary gone.

14

THEY let her go. Not only, I found, because of my going to Bailey, but because the children had talked about her and people were getting uneasy and restless. We had to take it and be quiet at Kerrin's rage when she came home confused with anger and humiliation. The days seemed a long series of unfought battles, a walking between poison-thorns, and there was a need for patience that wore the endurance raw. She hated me, could not help but feel that this came because of that morning I'd found her, and asked why I didn't take the place now I'd pried her from it. "I'd make a slow teacher, Kerrin," I told her. "I haven't the way with them you have." "Maybe you haven't," she said, "but the money would be the same—and yours. That's what you wanted, wasn't it?"

There was no use arguing with her any more, and she could not even work long at one thing. What we asked her to do we could have done ourselves with less time and worry. Father took it indifferently well.

He had the grace or fear not to taunt her with it, and gave up his anger at seeing her wander around and stare aimlessly when there was so much still to do and we could not trust her even to haul the water. It was hard to see her around because of feeling pity; she looked like a thing scratched down to bone, moved by a kind of sourceless energy, not of her own strength any more.

Grant was patient with her in those days, more than ever before. He worked, himself, with a kind of dogged steadiness that shuts out thought and feeling, and used to walk the six miles down to his father's farm more often, spending nights there and coming back at four in the morning.

The evenings were pale and drab now, and Merle never sang with him any more. Not that his voice was much good or with any tune, but it had a strong music to it, and mixed up with Merle's voice it seemed sort of beautiful to us. Even Father used to come sit and listen, and want more when they were sung out empty. Now that Grant went away so much he began to get restless and suspicious, and asked him once if he thought to get married soon; but when Grant said no and turned away, he never probed him again, and took his uneasiness out on other things, complaining of heat and the sores that came out on his neck and hands.

The dryness went on worse than ever now A quiet and monotonous dying. Fires started up in the brush, and there was dust over everything from the new road begun half a mile south of us. We could see the dust blowing up, and there was a sort of brown fog along the trees mixed with smoke from the woods burned back along the sides. Fires to the east and west of us had charred off acres, run through part of Rathman's land and killed what was left of his corn. Not that it mattered much,—blasted already and mouthed by grasshoppers. And now this to the south of us—a hot river of wind, constant and full of the black leaf-ash sometimes.

"Damn fools!" Father said. Over and muttering to himself, or breaking out to Mother: "Damn fools to fire now!" Only scrub-pasture and timber lay between us and the road, and it was like ploughing rock to make a furrow. The underbrush dry as sand.

"What do they want a new road for?" Merle said. "Wasn't the old one good enough? Couldn't you get to town on the old one just as well? What do they have to come burning and smoking and raising up dust like a cyclone for? It's enough to turn your stomach all over!"

"It's wider," Dad said; looked at her hard and suspiciously, and then over at Grant. "Ain't it a lot better, Grant?"

"A better *road,*" Grant said. He grinned and balanced his words between them so that neither could take him for their meaning.

"A farmer wants good roads," Father said.

"Good roads, maybe," Merle snapped at him, "but not to drive through a field of char. It's like a desert by day! Ask Grant—he knows, he has to haul. Why don't *you* haul by day if you like it so much?"

"There're worse things to get torn over," Grant said. "You can't hate everything and come out sane."

"I can," Merle answered him. "I can hate people, and heat, and selfishness, and this Goddamn dust, and farmers that starve their dogs and don't know how to feed their children, and lice, and those like you who stand around saying there isn't a use to try! I can hate about everything there is to hate, and not want to die either!" She looked up at Grant and stuck her big hands on her hips and grinned up at him, mad and good-natured and ready to splinter anything that he had to say. I saw his fingers tighten up in his fists to keep from touching her; then he turned away and went off to wash his face for excuse not to be near, and mumbled out of his towel that it was a good thing maybe she had so much work to do, and then something about setting all earth on end with her energy and go around chipping off mountain peaks for gravel.

She wouldn't let him get by with passing it over, as though he thought there were no use arguing with a child, and told him only a noisy hate—hate that got itself born in action—counted. "A man can be angry and rage inside," she told him, "but unless it comes up to the surface he might as well love what he hates!"

"—Or hate what he loves," Grant said. And I saw Kerrin watching them both.

Merle turned away at that and went out, and Grant did not follow her. . . . The air was a queer red fog from the sun and smoke, and she seemed the only clear and definite thing in all of the dusty smear and mist.

15

I DO not know how we should have gone on or how things would have been otherwise, but that night was end and beginning to more than I had thought possible to endure.

Kerrin saw the fire down in the south field. She had been out late, wandering around near the barns, and saw it blurring the line of scrub-oaks, and smelled it on the wind. She came back calling us out of sleep, half-wild with excitement. "It's come!" she shouted. Pounded against Grant's door, and shook Merle, lying heavy and sunk hours-under in sleep. Father stumbled out of his bed, and I woke up, not understanding, but saw her shrieking there in the moonlight, and even the red of her hair was plain—the night was so startlingly clear. "Get up, you poor fools!" she shouted, and seemed almost wildly happy in a malicious way. Grant came out, still strapping his clothes around him; he was grim and tired-looking, and his hair ragged. We could see the red light now, a wide wash of it along the field-edge, and the acrid smoke hot along the air. Grant was out first, running toward the barns, and then Father, stumbling and swearing, his face an awful muddle of fear and rage.

"You'll never be able to stop it now!" Kerrin shouted; then suddenly—and strangely, for her—she snatched at Mother and tried to hold her back. "Don't go!" she begged her.

"We have to," Mother said. "It's coming fast." She dragged down a pile of sacks, and Kerrin helped her. We soaked them wet in the last of the barrels, and it hurt to see water splash out along the floor.

The heat was terrible. We fought it along the edge where the bushes were low, but the smoke stung like wasps and poured out over us blind in clouds, and our skins got raw with the heat. I looked over at Merle once, flailing away with her sack, and the steam from it whirled around her as though she herself were a torch. The heat could have been borne, terrific and searing as it was, but the smoke didn't give us a chance to even endure it. Torture too crafty to fight. Kerrin ran back, covering her eyes, and screamed; and I remember now how awful her thin, frantic stumbling looked in the moonlight, but could hardly see for the tears stung out of my eyes; and beat blindly at the grass, feeling the hot ground underfoot, and heard all around the steady roar from the woods' edge where it was rushing over the dry oak leaves, and the dead underbrush was a mass of flames. "Don't let it reach the cornfield!" Dad kept shouting. He and Grant shoveled helplessly, trying to scrape out a path that the flames couldn't leap, and saw it sweep out beyond them, farther down, closing in on us with a great arc. There was no time for any thought, no time for fear. It was horrible, and too near for us even to realize what it meant.

Then suddenly—I don't know how, unless she stumbled and lurched sideways into the burning weeds—Mother fell and was lashed around with flames before she could drag herself up or scream. Grant saw her fall and ran half a field, throwing his shovel and shouting at us through the roar and smoke-haze, and when we reached them he had dragged her out beyond the fire, smothering the flames with his hands and the sack she'd held,—but too late to keep her from being burned.

Grant and Kerrin carried her back, but Dad stayed on in the field, lashing and digging like a giant, and Merle with him. I went back to the house, knowing that Kerrin would only cry and pray and not be able to find or know where anything was, nor did I know myself very well for the moment what I should do or find to help her. I sent Kerrin down to Rathmans' and did what I could with the things we had, but nothing seemed enough to cover all the terrible burns, and there was no more salve on the shelf than a little to spread on her face and hands.

The air was full of smoke and like a fog in the lamplight. It was hard to breathe now, and Mother cried out sometimes.

"You go back," I told Grant. There wasn't anything he could do,—no way for anyone to get between her and the suffering, and there was the fire coming on nearer all the time. Scrub-oaks and brush bursting suddenly into torches all up and down the field, the fence posts flaring up, and roar of sound when the branches crashed to earth. Grant went out, and I stayed alone, not able to do anything, only praying and crying out to something or against everything—Christ please!

It was awful—horrible—to see her suffering. I think I would rather be racked than go through that night again.—The red light reflected hot on the window-panes, the choking air, and Mother lying there on the bed, blotched red and half-crazy with pain. . . . Then Kerrin came back bringing some salve, and said they had called a doctor, and stood there crying and beat her hands together—even went down on her knees by the bed and kept saying—O God please take it away!—take it away! Mrs. Rathman looked at her, not understanding, and scared at her fierceness, and all the time the smoke was getting stronger and more acrid in the room till Mother started gasping for breath. Then Max came and Kerrin got up and went out with him to finish fighting a trench around the cornfield. The whole woods were almost gone now, and the haystack nearest the fence, and there was the hiss and lick of fire through the wheat stubble, creeping fast in a tongue across the northwest corner.

"You go too," Mrs. Rathman said. She spread out her slimy brown salve over Mother's neck, and seemed solid and comforting, full of assurance now that Kerrin was gone. I went out again and ran toward the field, saw them moving against the fire like furious black ants, Merle flailing and beating still, and the men digging wild as animals. Dad had no breath to speak when I got there, but looked up at me, his face angry and twisted with the pain, and then went on shoveling at the grass.

"Mrs. Rathman's here," I said, "and the doctor's coming." It was easier to stand the heat and smother of smoke than to see her suffer, and I beat at the shallow grass till it was torture to draw in breath.

When they came to the scraped-out path the flames stopped, licked and flickered and went out, but leaped beyond it in places and caught at the moulting thistles, rushing forward again and spreading out. It was like a terrible nightmare of earth's end. . . . Then suddenly the wind died down, the flames came slower, and smoke drifted up instead of coming in blind clouds. We saw the moon paler, and there was a greyish light. It was the hour before dawn when the wind had always stopped in those nights; and a faint chill was come at last in the air. In the gradual ceasing of sound we heard the cocks crow with a fresh eerie shrillness, startling as from another world.

We beat out the last flames and Merle covered a smouldering post with earth. The wires lay down across the field with the charred posts left at intervals like burned crows caught between the barbs.

16

IT WAS over, but there were still the black, ruined woods, the stakeless fence, and the great haystack gone. We looked at each other in the grey, sourceless light, and could not laugh,—though, God knows, when I think of it now I remember most clearly Max's swollen face spotted with purple from the heat, and his eyebrows singed, and Merle's legs black as the burned fields were, her hair singed too and hanging down like a mane around her big face. Father turned and shouted at us not to forget the shovels, and started limping off toward the house. Max came along, grumbling and swearing in a loud mutter, and rubbing his itching eyes until they were raw. We had no feeling of triumph or success; only of tiredness and the awful, unnecessary waste. It had cost too much to win.

I looked back once and saw the black, smouldering mess, and there was the crash of a dead branch falling, and the cinders rising up in a cloud around it. This behind us; and in front of us the fear for Mother, and everything blurred in an ache of tiredness. Father stumbled on ahead and I heard him muttering

Mother's name to himself, repeating it over like an oath or prayer, and once he blurted it out aloud when he blundered against a stone.

We saw the doctor had come and there was a lamp in her room, a drained and sickly yellow in the coming light outside. Father stopped at the door and took off his shoes, picking the buckets up as in a mechanical, meaningless rite. When the doctor came out, he went with him to the car and stood there a long time talking and listening, his eyes on the ground.

There were the cows still to be milked, everything still to be done. The sky cloudless, heat coming already in the air. The warm mugginess of sun through mist.—I went out in a daze of tiredness, but Kerrin was there already, quick and excited as if the fire had got inside her and behind her eyes, and she kept jerking her arms around and shouting at the horses. She started to let them out, and I told her that Dad might need them today. Then she turned and howled about having to give the horses water, although there was none in the pasture where she was driving them. I went out to shut the gate and came back and saw Grant fumbling at a rope, with one hand trying to unfasten it, the other stuck out stiff, black except for the fence-tear ripped across it. Kerrin was with him, and what happened came so swiftly that it was like a quick fierce vision more than a thing that was real. She pried at the knot he couldn't loosen, but it was pulled too hard, and then grabbed at his knife and hacked the knot loose with a ragged sawing. Grant snatched at her hand to stop her. "Don't ruin the rope," he warned. "—You'll cut yourself!"

She jerked back from him, his hand on her wrist, with the knife still clenched in her fingers, then suddenly twisted her arm behind her so that his own followed and all her thin, dangling body was pressed up hard against him, one arm over his shoulders and her face in his black, scarred neck. I could see Grant's face and the swift look on it, and then in less than the time of seeing he dropped her wrist and she fell back, but still with one hand on his arm and the knife clenched hard in the other. I looked up and saw Father standing in the door, his face still red and wild-looking from the fire, purple-spotted and flushed, and his hair singed across where a branch had struck it.

"What're you doing there?" he shouted. "Why ain't you working, Grant? What're you doing there with Kerrin?"

"Saving a rope," Grant said and laughed. He would have said more, but Kerrin suddenly clenched his arm and, half-turning, hurled the knife at Father, all the old hate come to her eyes again, and screaming out words that I'd heard only once in life before. The knife went wide, struck slant-wise against the wall and fell back in the dust.

Now remembering what happened, looking back on it in these four months' time, through the blur of all that has come to us since, everything seems like a dusty smear of feet, and Father lurching toward Kerrin, and Grant's arm against him, knocking him back against the wall, and Kerrin's high voice,—"You kill him, Grant!"—and then Grant standing back, not touching Father and shouting at her to go and get out fast. Then Kerrin running—not because she was afraid of Father, being beyond fear, and everything swallowed up by hate—but because of the sound—the cold, fierce ring in Grant's voice. She ran past Father, slumped down panting where the harness hung, and I saw her hand dart down and snatch something off the floor.

Father straightened up and went out back toward

the house, not following Kerrin, but as if he'd forgotten why he'd come.

Grant picked up the rope and threw it away. "What'll she do now, Marget?" he asked me, and started searching along the wall for the knife.

"She took it," I told him; and Grant saw what I thought but didn't say. We went out after her then, Grant half-dragging me over the stones. I was too tired to think or care, but knew that there was this to be done and followed him, feeling his heavy hand more than either the sun or fear.

17

WHEN I remembered it afterward and the thought had grown more accustomed through necessity, and the need to keep a hard layer of calmness between me and the dark that kept coming up like a tide, I was glad this had happened when it did, and I knew after all that her death was the one good thing God did. There was no place for her. If we had had money, we might have sent her away. She never belonged with us, and maybe there is no place on earth for people like her. I was glad she had died. I could not feel any other way about it. Something had hardened and dried up in me in those last few months. Something that had been hardening before, all through the rest of our pinched and scrawling life.

It was the way we found her and the awful completeness of death that came as a shock. It was the first time I had ever seen Kerrin quiet. Even in sleep she used to move and twist like a restless snake, and when awake her hands and eyes were never still. Twitching and moving back and forth. But now she was absolutely quiet. . . . We found her back of the sheep barn and near the water-trough. It was after a long time of searching, and sometimes Grant called her but there was no answer, and we began to think she had gone off in the woods when suddenly we came on her lying against the barn wall, with one arm fallen across the trough, and the blood from her wrist staining the shallow water.

Grant knelt down by her and then looked up. She was dead already, and her skin drawn tight as paper over her cheeks. So thin it was almost like finding the hard bones of her, and the rest gone to dust already. I could not cry; but Grant's face was less hard, and when he picked her up there was no disgust or shrinking in it, and he carried her as he would have carried a child or a little hound.

Dad took it hard. More for the swift, spectacular way she had done it, outraging decency and precedent, than because of any belated love. If he saw this as a last desperate taunt or felt himself at all to blame, he did not show it. He was out in the barn again when we came back, milking with a dogged steadiness. He had eaten nothing and washed only his hands, huge and red like gloves on the end of his blackened arms. "Get out," he mumbled at Grant, then saw what it was he carried. "Who did this, Marget?" he kept asking. "What happened to her?" He could not believe she had killed herself. A raw, unnatural thing. A thing no girl had a right to do. Then he turned toward Grant and accused him of betraying her. Worked himself up in a terrible rage. But Grant was quiet, listened to him as to a furious child, and when he was through asked if he thought that Mrs. Haldmarne should know or if we could keep it from her.

"Don't tell her," I said. "Not unless she asks."

"What d'ya mean?" Father said, loud but not shouting any more. "Ain't she a right to know about her own children? Ain't she a right to know what's been going on?" Then suddenly he changed and sat down. "Go on—do what you want. Lie to her. I don't care. Get me some food, Marget; I ain't coming in to eat."

Merle cried, but was not afraid to touch her. She combed Kerrin's messy red hair and covered her wrists with a towel. We did not tell Mother. She was too blind and sick to come see her anyway, and had not even noticed the doctor's coming.

Late in the day the coroner had come, but she did not notice him either.

"Kerrin was sick," I told the man, "—sick in her head. She'd been that way a long time. It was the fire and Mother's being burned and her thinking that Mother was going to die that made her do it."

Father didn't say anything much, but sat and looked at the man, sullenly and defying him to find out more. Grant sat near Merle and watched him writing the paper out: *Kerrin Haldmarne . . . dead of her own hand. . . . Admitted suicide.* Once Grant turned and looked at Merle sitting there serious and unconscious of him as though he were not there, intent only on seeing the paper signed, all of us exonerated and free of scandal or law. Grant looked at her, and then down at his hands; and I heard his voice again in my mind, the sound of it pushed unexpectedly from him in despair one night.—"Marget, isn't there anything I can do? It's like being half-crucified sometimes!" How could I tell him who knew one answer only?

Outside was the hot windless air, the dead elm branch against the sky, and the point of a buzzard drifting. Even then out of old habit my eyes went searching for clouds. And here in the hot still room—all of us sitting embarrassed, hating this man who neither believed us nor was able to prove a lie. Then at last he got up and stuffed his papers away, and Merle asked him if he would have anything to eat, hating him but knowing what Mother would have done. He said yes,—if it made no trouble. "No trouble," Merle said. "It's already made." She pulled the coffee-pot off the stove and cut him some cake. It was dark and crumbling, and she ate a sliver herself, absently, licking the crumbs from her palm, then handed some over to Grant, looking at him, her eyes impersonal and yet with a kind of pity. Grant took a thin piece but only rubbed it together in his hand. There was something ghastly and unreal about it all, like a funeral supper or a wake. I wished to God that the man would get out and go.

He ate two pieces, and I could not help thinking of how the molasses was nearly gone already, and only a little sugar left, and I hated him for eating our food. "Thanks," he said to Merle, got up and wiped his mouth. We made him nervous, sitting around this way. Nobody said anything much but Merle, and once Father asked him if corn might be going up. "Don't know, that's not my line," he answered. "It's high enough now for the ones that have to buy. You farmers have got stuff to eat anyway. That's something, ent it?"

He left at last, and by the time he was gone there was the milking to start again, and supper still to be gotten; and there was relief in doing these stale and familiar things.

18

KERRIN was buried up in the old Haldmarne lot. There was no funeral, thank God.

The night after she was buried, Grant came down while I was watering the sheep. He stood there watching and seemed a little at peace. It was quiet and getting dark. Then he spoke suddenly and with anger, watching the small dust under their feet. "Remember what Merle said about Max once?—that he liked to be with the sheep and hogs because they were things that were even more stupid than himself? That's why I like it, I guess. There's a mild irony in being wiser than sheep, at least."

"There's more than that to it, Grant," I said. "More for *you,* anyway—" It seemed an empty and obvious thing to say. Of no help. But I had never seen him like this before. Grant had never been arrogant, but had never before been so bitter at himself. It made me afraid, because he seemed to make of himself another and lesser man. And I wanted to believe in his strength, to feel that somewhere things were all right. I didn't want to believe what I knew.

"They trust you; there's a healing in that," I told him.

"They'd trust anything," Grant said. "Anything that's human."

I wished he would go and get out of sight. Stop being there, so near that I almost stumbled against him with the bucket, but all of a life away.

Then he told me he was leaving for good next week.

"On account of Dad?" I asked him.

"More on account of Merle," he said.

I asked him where he would go. I can hear the words now,—quiet, standing off by themselves, having nothing to do with my hot, sick heart. "Where will you go, Grant? What will Dad do?"

"I'll go back up-state," he said. "Find a place somewhere. Max'll come back and help you. He's out of a job again."

"Max made a good worker sometimes," I said. I dribbled out the last bucket and hung it on the nail. I could not say "God keep you!" It kept getting darker there near the stalls, and something in me cracking and straining, wanting to do what Kerrin had done, forget everything else and do just that, touch him and get what sour comfort there'd be in this;—and there was the awful love, the desire shut back, sick in the throat. . . . Let me go—let me out!—O God please! . . . and the mind sitting there cold and hard and yet fearful: You can't do this . . . you can't do it . . . you can't.—It's a lie that the body is a prison! It's the mind, I tell you!—always the cold, strong mind that's jailer. I felt something hammering in my throat, and my hands were shaking together like old leaves. I ran out through the shed and left him. I don't know what he thought. I was crying, and it hurt to cry. I was sick and hating because I loved him.

19

THE day that Grant left was like all the rest. Dust and heat and the ugliness of dying maples. I told myself I was glad he was going. That there was a dignity in death. This half-life was too much to bear, the shame of betrayal too much to fear. I would rather have died than have them find out how much I loved him. . . . This was a foolish pride. Who was I, after all, that it made any difference what I thought? What had I to hold inviolate? . . . Now there'll be peace, I told myself. I can learn to accept, feel free to begin again and rebuild life on something else, on something more than the sight of him, which had been a bitter sufficiency until then. I must have been dried with drouth. I couldn't feel any more those days. I'd see things and do them and see sometimes the look on Grant's face when he talked to Merle. I'd think—he's going next week; but it was as if I was thinking of someone else, known by name only and no concern of mine. Father said he was glad Grant was going, and that he could manage well enough by himself. He knew that this was a lie, but pretended it for the sake of some dignity, and in himself dreaded being alone with us again.

Grant did the milking that night, and came on the porch to say goodbye while Father was out in the dairy.—There were things, I suppose, I could have said. But I felt like a stranger suddenly, and as though Grant had never spoken to me of his loving Merle or any of all the things we had talked about.

"Where's Merle, Marget?" he asked; and then, "Never mind, don't call her." He put out his hand in an awkward, formal way, but laughed. "Goodbye, Marget," he said. "I hope to God your mother is better soon!"

"She'll be," I said. "I don't ever doubt it, Grant." I thought that I said, "Come back when you can," but must only have felt the words. Grant stood there looking down at me with his old kindly smile, supposing I had started to speak but never finished. Then, when I only stood there, he put out his hand again.

"No farmer's ever going to have a soft time," he said, "but I wish it would come out easier for you."

"We'll get along," I told him. "It's a pleasanter way of losing money than most."

He laughed and went out, but stopped by the gate where Merle was. She turned and went down the fence-row with him toward the road, and he waved his hat once before they got out of sight.

I went inside and stared at the jelly-glasses and around the room, and picked up a ball of dust near the table-leg, seeing them plainly and not at all. Then I went back to Mother's room when I heard her speak.

PART THREE YEAR'S END

HE WAS gone and I had to accept this, take it hard to myself and stop suffering. One doesn't die of loss. Only a part dies.

The fifth month of the drouth began with nothing but clouds and the taunt of an hour's drizzle. Nothing to soak the ground below an inch deep. September now and the fields more barren than in winter. The pastures where mules and hogs had been not even covered with dying grass. They were eaten to earth and looked like the hide of a mangy hound. Even the ironweed was withered. For a mile around there was nothing but ragweed in the fields, dust-green and heavy-pollened. Locust trees in the south woods died together. Small gold leaves sifted down and were covered with dust. A weird sick acre full of the dying twisted trees, and underneath them the dying ironweed-stalks. The dead elm leaves hung like folded bats.

Mother got neither better nor worse. She just went on suffering. I do not think the doctor knew very much. When her skin turned black in one place, he began to look worried. "If she's healed," Merle said, "it'll come more of her own will than out of this stuff he uses." We hadn't the money to pay anyone else even if there had been anyone else to come. I used to sit up at night beside her, and at first it was almost too hard. It was awful—the pain she suffered. Hours and days of agony enough to turn her mind, and yet she seldom said anything aloud. I thought sometimes I should scream out myself, suffering for her and half-crazy with pity and helplessness. But there is a merciful blind skin that comes over the heart at times. You can endure this much, and after that there come intervals of hardness. She would get well. I could believe nothing else, nor let myself pity or fear for her. Somehow I trusted that her death was a thing that could never come to us. The doctor said there was hope, and there were days when we thought she looked better and the burns seemed to cause less pain. There was no doubt, no fear in her own mind. She talked about what we would do this winter when there was less of the work outside.

Our life seemed only a long waiting for her to get well—a vacuum in which we moved and did things, but nothing was the same. I felt lost and Merle seemed suddenly grown older, as if waked from a living sleep. Not Grant's love or Kerrin's death had changed her as much as this. She missed Grant, but only as someone to tilt against. Missed his dry and gritty humor. She knew why he'd gone and had never been quite so placid and easy after that night of the fire. But she did too much else to brood over this, and her mind was too full of Mother to leave any room for the thought of him. I say this, not knowing, but only as it seemed.—One night she walked for hours over the place and came back angry and restless still, which was strange for her who had only to smash up kindling and haul it in, to rid herself of these mind-swarmed gnats. "It's the dust—the damn dust— It gets in your marrow almost," she said. "There's nothing left even to look at now!"

Father was pitiful in a way. He asked, "How is she?" each morning, and almost demanded with his eyes that we say she was well—entirely recovered. I think he expected it every morning. "No better" or "Just the same," Merle would say, and he'd go out looking as though we'd betrayed him in some way.

The days were quiet with Kerrin and Grant gone. Only by getting away from the house and off in the fields sometimes could I keep sane and find life bearable. It was not a healing;—neither from earth nor love nor from any one thing alone comes healing,—

but without this I should have died. If I'd screamed and shrieked out that I couldn't bear it, they would have thought I'd gone mad; but it's the silence that's really madness, the holding quiet, holding still, going on as if everything were the same. There was no one to talk to. I could not add my own fear to Merle's, nor could we talk about Grant.

2

I WENT one night up to the pond in the north pasture. It was hot again even in the nights. The warm air was tired and dull, and it took a long time for the south wind to bring any coolness. It was a moon night and the stars pale. Even the constellations dim. I could see the dust on the leaves and feel it deep around my feet in the road. The corn-stalks looked like white skeletons. I remembered in a wasteful and sentimental way the nights I had come along this road and up through the drying pawpaw thicket with Grant. There was no touch of his to remember,—only his words; and words are cold, tomb-like things, lasting longer perhaps than even the strongest and most fierce touch, but stony things. There was little that

Grant hadn't seen or heard, and he used to talk a great deal because I was hungry to learn and know. I could remember these things, and the sound, heavy and blurring, of his voice, but they were no consolation now. The awful loneliness was worse than even in the first days when he was gone. . . . I went up and stood and stared at the water, black and moon-webbed, and the frog eyes coming out like sparks near the edge. It was shrunken, and slime over part.

. . . There ought to be some way of putting yourself beyond pain. The days did it mostly, but it crept back and crawled up in darkness, thrust in hard when light was gone. I could sleep, and in the morning wake up and think "Tonight I can sleep again"—but this was no way to live!—the days only deserts crossed between night and night. I sat on the pond-edge and tried to think it out clearly but couldn't, and only wondered if Dad would remember the stalls tomorrow or if I would have to tell him again, and if the pole-beans were too dry, and if we killed one of Merle's geese how long it would last. I argued a long time with the doctor in my mind. I gave him five geese and the promise of a calf if it ever came. He kept refusing, and I carried on the long stupid conversation, staring at the pond and knowing all the time I would pay him in money anyway and never mention even potatoes for exchange. Then I remembered the night I had come up here in April, six months ago. I could have laughed almost, thinking of my mild and foolish excitement then. "This year will be better . . different!"—I took a wry pleasure in the irony of it.

But after a while the whiteness and the night wind had made me feel more still. Almost at peace. Almost as though all these things were behind me.—Big poisoned shadows in a dream now finished.

I came back late and saw the light still in the window of Mother's room, and came near and heard that sharp, awful sound she made sometimes, like a needle thrust out from her throat. And everything was the same. Real and unfinished and still to be lived on through.

3

THE assessor came in October on a day when Dad was out ploughing an acre down near the creek-bottom where ground was something beside rock-dust. He had too much to do now that Grant was gone, but had asked no one else to help. "I can manage," he told me. "Everything's dead anyway. Only the cows to do." The truck-garden looked like a graveyard with all the things still unburied, but there was still more than enough of work. He didn't seem able to concentrate or decide what he wanted to do. Things took him twice as long. "I got to whitewash," he'd said that morning, spent half an hour getting his stuff together, then left it to plough this acre.

—Braille, the man said his name was. Brought us the papers to be filled. "You've got a lot of good land," he told us. A big bald man with a nervous cackle and a kind enough way. "A good house, too." Dad listed his cows and horses, and they sounded a lot written down. The plows and tractor . . . a hundred sheep . . . nine hogs . . . a hundred chickens. . . . "Where's your car?" Braille wanted to know. Wouldn't believe Dad when he said there wasn't any. "You folks are pretty well off," he said. Looked at the orchard and the barns.

"Pretty well *out,*" Dad said. "Them barns are empty. That silo's only three-quarter full. I have to *buy* feed this winter. I borrowed two hundred to fix this dairy up, and have to pay you because it is, and make less than that off it a month."

"It ain't encouraging," the man said. "I saw a mule out there in the pasture you didn't list."

"He ain't mine!" Dad shouted. "I'm pasturing him for Rathman."

"I reckon you don't use him either?" Braille said. Looked at Dad and winked one eye. "Last farmer I visited had four strays,—just passin' through, he said, and he let 'em graze.—Maybe I'll drop around next week and see if they passed on yet!"

Dad didn't laugh. "I ain't got any money to pay taxes with," he said. "You're wasting your time with all those figgers."

"Where'd your school be?" Braille wanted to know. "Where'd your roads be if nobody wanted to pay?"

Dad spread out his hands and hunched his shoulders. "I don't know, man!" he said. "I don't care much now. All I want is a chance to live without shoveling out everything I can earn. What're all these things worth?" He pointed around at the farm. "They don't bring in what they cost!"

"You want'm, don't you?" Braille asked. "Ain't this where you want to live?—Well, you got to pay for it then."

"You talk like living was sort of a sin," Merle burst out. "Something a man had to do penance for!"

Braille looked blank as a board and shook his head. "No crime," he said. "You just got to pay, that's all."

"You get me some money," Father said, "and I will. If a man's no income, how's he going to pay property-taxes?"

"I guess he can't," Braille said. "But he's got to." He rolled up his papers and got in the car. "Goodbye, you folks," he said. "I got it all down, I reckon."

"I reckon you have," Merle answered. "I never would have believed we owned so much. It makes a man count his blessings!"

Braille grinned and drove off. He seemed a kind enough man. Not steel. Not a man intended to leave a trail of sick hate wherever he went.

Father stood staring after him, and then wandered off to the barn, talking and jerking at the bucket. It was awful to see him that way. Father once so sure of himself if nothing else,—now not fighting back any more. Fussing instead of storming, now. Wasting himself in petty hates, and riddled with worry.

4

HE SOLD most of the steers next week, hoping to make the taxes that way; and besides, the pastures were all gone dead. They weren't very fat, and we had to pay Max to take them in, and a lot went for express. If we'd bought them to fatten we would have lost everything; as it was, we got barely enough to buy soap and nails. I thought—and hoped—that Dad would break out in a shouting rage the night he added up his accounts. He had sunk so deep in himself that it would have been a relief to hear him roar out or swear. But everything went in—the whole storm—inside himself. He chucked the book in the drawer and went outside to the barn.

Mother asked what had happened; she could tell by his walk alone how furious he was. I told her, but not everything. "He got less than he thought to," I said.

Mother moved her hand in a painful, impatient way. "Why don't you say the rest, Marget? How much did he lose?"

"We made two dollars," Merle told her, "off nineteen steers. The cattle-business is very good. Next year we might try twenty and buy a big dish-mop in the fall."

Mother looked worried. Her mind wandered off in a web of pain sometimes and she did not bother much over things, but she seemed clear and too able to suffer for other people that night. "Get him to rest more," she said. "He's too wound up. Work brings so little anyway. He'll see that sometime. . . . Does he eat enough?"

He ate pretty well, I told her. Didn't add that there wouldn't be much *to* eat after a while.

She didn't seem satisfied, but was too tired to talk any more. "Tell him to rest," she said again, and then was quiet, staring out of the window.

5

SHE died that night. It was early in October a month ago, and the autumn storms began. The first rains since February. . . . Once I thought there were words for all things except love and intolerable beauty. Now I know that there is a third thing beyond expression—the sense of loss. There are no words for death.

The night after her funeral I went out and walked miles in the dark. It was cold and damp. Fog-chillness and the air like a winter marsh. Leaves wet in the wagon-ruts. I don't know how far I went—hours along the dim roads; but this time the dark could not cover or fill the broken emptiness. I could not pretend or hope any longer, or believe blindly in any goodness. It was all gone. Faith swept away like a small mound of grass, and nothing to live or wait for any longer. God was only a name, and it was her life that had been the meaning of that name. Now there was nothing left. . . . There was a night eight or nine years ago when there had come for the first time a shadow of this great loss and doubt, and I remembered it now, stumbling back through the useless dark. I had overheard them talking one night, Dad tired and exasperated, his corn gone at less than the price of a plough. "God! don't they *want* a man to farm?" he said. "Where they think corn's going to come from after they pry us off the land? They've got to eat, God knows!" . . . And then Mother's voice, fierce and half-crying in the dark: "Let'm have pig-weed and cockle! That'll grow wild." I was afraid of the sound in her voice. It was as if all her trust and belief were snatched away, and left us grappling with wind and emptiness, and she, like the rest of us, was come down to hate and doubt. I waited to hear her say something else, say that it didn't matter, tell him next year would come out better . . . but she was quiet and didn't say anything more at all. I saw partly then what was plain to me now in this night after her burial—that I had believed because she had, and if she lost it and came to the darkness where we were, groping along with no more light than I,—then all of my blind belief in goodness was gone. . . . But all this was nothing beside the unbearable feeling of loss.

6

. . . IT IS almost two months now since her death, and we have gone on living. It is November and the year dying fast in the storms. The sycamores wrenched of leaves and the ground gold. The ploughed fields scarred around us on the hills. We have had our mortgage extended, but it does not mean that we are free or that much is really changed. Only a longer time to live, a little longer to fight, fear shoved off into an indefinite future.

I do not see in our lives any great ebb and flow or rhythm of earth. There is nothing majestic in our living. The earth turns in great movements, but we jerk about on its surface like gnats, our days absorbed and overwhelmed by a mass of little things—that confusion which is our living and which prevents us from being really alive. We grow tired, and our days are broken up into a thousand pieces, our years chopped into days and nights, and interrupted. Our hours of life snatched from our years of living. Intervals and things stolen between—between what?—those things which are necessary to make life endurable?—fed, washed, and clothed, to enjoy the time which is not washing and cooking and clothing. . . . Thoreau was right. He was right even as Christ was right in saying *Be ye also perfect.*—And as beyond us.

We have no reason to hope or believe, but do because we must, receiving peace in its sparse moments of surrender, and beauty in all its twisted forms, not pure, unadulterated, but mixed always with sour potato-peelings or an August sun.

There is no question of what we will do. It is as plain before us as the dead fields. We are not trapped any more than all other men. Any more than life itself is a trap. How much of what came to us came of ourselves? Was there anything that we could have done that we did not do? God—if you choose to say that the drouth is God—against us. The world against us, not deliberately perhaps, more in a selfish than malicious way, coming slowly to recognize that we are not enemies or plough-shares. And we against ourselves. It is not possible to go on utterly alone. Father may see this now, in a furious and tardy recognition. We can go forward; the way is plain enough. But it is only that this road has too high banks and too much dust. . . .

7

I WENT over to Rathmans' this morning. It is eight months since that time when I went in May, envying them mildly and full of a foolish hope. But now there is neither hope nor envy left.

Lena behaved herself better, the old lady told me. But she did not seem happy. "Come in and see Papa," she said. Old Rathman lay there on his red blanket, shriveled up like a pod. His eyes were dim and cauled over, but he knew me for a while. "Pop sees you go by for the mail," Mrs. Rathman told me. "He knows you sometimes when he ain't out of his head."

"I came over to get some eggs," I told him. "Our hens aren't laying much just now. Nobody's are."

"Nobody's are," he repeated after me. "Nobody's got anything. You're young, though—you ain't like me. You can do things still. You ain't just lying here, old like me . . . fit for nothin' . . . I can't do nothin'. . . ." He said it over and over like an old lesson,—forgot I was there and turned his head away. I could hear him muttering and tossing when we left the room.

"He's real clear sometimes," Mrs. Rathman said. "It's his shouting makes Lena mad." She got me the eggs, but wouldn't take any money. "Just bring some over when you can." She came to the door with me and smiled kind of greyly, her round face patient and resigned. "Maybe there'll be a better year next. Things don't come twice this way. . . ."

Then I came out of the hot kitchen and walked back up the road. The hounds howling and strangling on their chains might have been the same as the ones we were afraid of as children. Everything might have been the same as in that time,—the white geese and the beagle hounds . . . the cabbage-heads sunk in the furrows . . . Max's car there, long, grey and wastefully big . . . the pumpkins set out in the arbor on a stool, for sale, but with no sign. A cat ran out of the dead lilac bushes and hid under the porch. I remembered and saw us again as we used to come up the road on the way to the mail, Kerrin ahead like a long red crane, her black stockings hanging wrinkled and dirty, and her long neck stretched out, singing some wild, sentimental song; and Merle and I stumbling along after, not hurrying, kicking stones and stopping to sow dried thistle-seeds, scattering them thoughtfully and without malice over the fall-ploughed earth. And then walking fast and uneasily by the house for fear the old man would see us and make us stop to talk, saying things that we could not understand or were slow to answer, afraid of his mocking look and cackle. . . .

I came back to where Father was still sitting as I had left him, the walnuts piled around him on the chopping-block. He turned and peered up when I came, with the old suspicious look, as though denying something not yet said, but smiled in a bleak and frozen way.

"Button your coat up, Marget," he said. "It's colder than you think. Damp-cold." He looked older in the light, so aged that he seemed almost to be Old Rathman there, pounding the black shells with his rheumy hands.

I pulled my coat up around me, although the air seemed mild with a kind of dull softness in it. "Merle'll make you a cake of those," I said. "She's going to be glad to see them shelled."

"She ought," Dad said. "It's hard work enough. . . . Hard work enough. . . ." He kept muttering this to himself in the same way that Old Rathman had done,—like a living parody of the other old man lying useless in his bed. And I saw Father with awful clearness as he would be soon. Old and querulous and able only to shell beans in the sun. And I saw how the debt would be Merle's and mine to carry by ourselves —how many years I do not know, but for a long and uncounted time. All life perhaps. . . . But I went on past him and up to the hill-edge where we used to peer down on the orchard when it looked like a gulf of clouds in spring. Now there were only the dry grey-orange branches blown back and forth like bushes in the wind, but still beautiful in the clean sharp way of winter things. And there was the cold fire of the oak trees, not fallen yet, and a kind of icy red along the woods.

Love and the old faith are gone. Faith gone with Mother. Grant gone. But there is the need and the desire left, and out of these hills they may come again. I cannot believe this is the end. Nor can I believe that death is more than the blindness of those living. And if this is only the consolation of a heart in its necessity, or that easy faith born of despair, it does not matter, since it gives us courage somehow to face the mornings. Which is as much as the heart can ask at times.